WHAT COMES AFTER

DEATH IS ONLY THE BEGINNING.

WHAT COMES AFTER

A NOVEL

CAREN HAHN

What Comes After by Caren Hahn

Published by Seventy-Second Press

www.carenhahn.com

Copyright © 2022 Caren Hahn

All rights reserved.

No part of this publication may be reproduced, distributed, or transmitted in any form or by any means, including photocopying, recording, or other electronic or mechanical methods, without the prior written permission of the publisher, except in the case of brief quotations embodied in critical reviews and certain other noncommercial uses permitted by United States of America copyright law and fair use.

ISBN-13: 978-1-958609-00-2

This is a work of fiction. Any references to historical events, real people, or real places are used fictitiously. Names, characters, places, and incidents either are the products of the author's imagination or are used fictitiously.

Cover design by Andrew Hahn.

Cover photo by Tyler Mode Media.

Edited by Rachel Pickett.

Printed in the USA

*In memory of Cami, whose 'after' came far too soon.
If she's not solving mysteries and having adventures in the
afterlife, I'm going to be deeply disappointed.*

BOOKS BY CAREN HAHN

MYSTERY:

What Comes After

THE OWL CREEK MYSTERIES

Smoke over Owl Creek

Hunt at Owl Creek

FANTASY:

THE WALLKEEPER TRILOGY

Burden of Power

Pain of Betrayal

Gleam of Crown

HATCHED

Hatched: Dragon Farmer

Hatched: Dragon Defender

Visit carenhahn.com to receive a free copy of

Charmed: Tales from Quarantine and Other Short Fiction.

WHAT COMES AFTER

CAREN HAHN

One

Death isn't what you think it is. I've been dead for three years, and it's nothing like I expected. I say three years, but of course that's in mortal terms. We still measure our time that way even though we don't age. We have seasons, but they're artificial. Nothing ever dies or grows. It just is. But it's hard to let go of the golden beauty of autumn or the pristine awe of a fresh blanket of snow. And really, who doesn't like summer?

So we hang onto our seasons even though they don't mark the passage of time the way they do for you. Instead, they're just trappings for our world: a strange and beautiful world that reminds us of what we lost and hints at what's to come.

What is to come?

No one really knows. I've talked to hundreds of people, maybe even thousands. None of them can tell me, because they're all stuck here too. But I've seen it done. When someone is ready to pass, it's like you can see every wonderful moment they've ever had shining in their eyes. They practically glow with it. This can go on for minutes or for days. Everyone gathers around to say their goodbyes, and we watch as the light inside of them brightens until it consumes them. And then they're gone. We look around and see joy reflected in each other's eyes, and we know that someday it will be our turn.

Someday, when we've learned to let go.

"This is beautiful, Lorna."

"Thank you." I fidget in my chair. Not because I'm physically uncomfortable, but because it's an ingrained habit from a lifetime of mortality. I cross my legs and tug at my pant leg, just as I would have done when I had a tangible body.

"I'm curious why you wanted to describe our world." Teresa is a short young woman with skin the color of the smooth buckeyes that I loved to gather as a child. Her tight curls are pulled out of her face with a wide elastic, and when she smiles, her whole face lights up in a way that makes me smile too. I wonder what Teresa was like as a mortal, but I'm not here to talk about Teresa's life. That's between Teresa and her therapist.

She's still waiting for an answer.

"Just thinking about it, I guess."

"Have you been thinking about passing on?"

I shrug. "Isn't that the point?"

"This is the first sign I've seen that you've been curious about it. How do you feel when you think about it?"

"I don't know. Nervous, I suppose. But also excited.

They always seem happy to go. So it must be a good thing, right?"

Teresa fingers the long gold necklace draped over the front of her pale cream blouse. "As far as we know, yes. That's why we're here."

"I just wish I knew if I could see them when I pass on."

"Your family?"

I nod. "Writing letters like this is nice, and I suppose I could still do that if I passed on, right? I mean, it's not like these ones get to them anyway. They're just glorified journal entries. But to actually see them and know what they're doing...Mindi will be graduating from high school next year. I don't want to miss that."

"And you think you might miss it if you pass on?"

"Can you tell me I won't?" I challenge.

Teresa holds my gaze and shakes her head. "Here's what I do know. Everyone I know who's passed on loved their kids as much as you love Mindi and Alex. Letting go doesn't mean forgetting. It doesn't mean they don't still miss them."

"Then what does it mean?"

Teresa's dark eyes look thoughtful. "If I knew, I wouldn't still be here, would I?"

I walk out of Teresa's office into the bright sunlight of a crisp autumn day. After three years, I no longer instinctively put on a sweater when a cool breeze blows. If I wear a sweater it's because I choose to, not because the weather dictates it. Sometimes I wear one on a blistering summer day, just because I can.

"I know that look."

I smile even before I turn to greet the man bounding down the steps toward me.

"What look?"

"You're going to the Memory Bank, aren't you?" Reif asks, one eyebrow cocked in an accusation.

"I hadn't decided, but now that you mention it..."

"Nope. No memories for you. Let's go get a coffee."

I grin. "I've seen people held back for lots of things. Children. Money. Failure. Regret. Even pets. You're the only one I know who can't pass on because he won't give up his coffee."

"Really? I'll bet it's what got most of these people out of bed every morning when they were alive. You'd think more of them would mourn it properly." He looks around the green space where people are milling about, sitting on benches or sunning on the grass. Two teenagers throw rocks into a pond, trying to hit the other bank. It's a scene of perfect tranquility, but Reif's brow is creased into a frown above his blue eyes.

"Why would we need coffee when we don't even need sleep?" I object. "If giving up coffee means I never have to be tired again, it's a trade I'm happy to make."

"You never were a purist, though. A true connoisseur would never think coffee was just about the energy boost."

"Give yourself a couple more years and then see what you think."

Reif only arrived six months earlier. The first words

he asked me were, "Do you know if this place has a Starbucks?" When I told him that without bodies there was no need for food or drink, he responded with, "You mean after all those years of weekly Mass I ended up in Hell after all?"

I didn't mind giving up all those "pleasures of the flesh" as Reif calls them (always with his eyebrows raised suggestively). Food, sleep, sex...I feel so much freer without them that within only a few months of being here they diminished to a distant dream. But that isn't the case with everyone. Some people will visit the Memory Bank just so they can torture themselves reliving a particularly gratuitous moment of their history. It never works that way, though. As immersive as it is to visit old memories, it isn't truly living them, and I always feel a little hollow and empty when I'm finished.

Yet somehow that's where I always want to go after therapy.

"Just one."

We stand outside the Memory Bank, its polished glass doors reflecting a cascade of golden leaves glittering around us.

"You'll regret it."

"Nah."

"You will. You'll get all sad and wish you could cry but without tears you won't feel any better."

I glare at Reif. "You haven't known me long enough to know how I feel."

He laughs. "Six months in this place is like an eternity. I know you better than I know my own sister. Come on, let's go take flying lessons."

"We can't fly," I say, annoyed. He already knows this.

"What's the point of not being able to die if we can't fly?"

"We're already dead! You really have no understanding of what we're doing here, do you? I swear, Reif, it's no wonder you can't pass on."

"Do you think I can fly after I pass on? That just might be worth giving up coffee. Come on, let's go check out the Arrivals."

He grabs my elbow and tugs gently, sending a buzz like a pinched nerve up my arm. It's hard to break these habits from mortality, so easy to forget that touch is another thing we lost. I join him, knowing that I can return later. Reif won't always be there to distract me.

I follow him to the plaza at the bottom of the hill where the newcomers arrive. Dozens of gates circle a large courtyard, their tall pillars glowing white with each Arrival. People gather around each one, waiting to greet friends and family mere seconds after they've died.

The gate nearest us is surrounded by a large crowd, their skin varying shades from dark to light but many of them sporting the same broad nose and round eyes. They're chatting excitedly, beaming at each other. I feel a twinge of jealousy as their skin takes on a sheen. I've seen this before. Whole families who wait to pass on until the last child or cousin or sibling joins them and they can all pass together.

A gray-haired woman materializes in the gate, stooped and bent with age. She scarcely glimpses the crowd waiting for her when her face lights up with such joy that years fall away with her smile. Within moments, she and the crowd gathered near her all glow with a transcendent light. It overwhelms my vision and I have to turn away. When the light ebbs, the whole family is gone.

"Wow," Reif says. "That's the most I've ever seen pass at once."

But my attention is caught by a girl who has appeared in the neighboring gate, a look of pure terror on her face. She stumbles backward, gasping. I step forward, then pause, looking around.

"Where's her Greeter?" I nudge Reif.

He shakes his head. "She looks pretty skittish. And young, too. What do you think, seventeen?"

"I'm going to talk to her."

"Good idea. I'll catch up with you later."

He jogs away and I hurry over to the girl. She leans against a pillar, looking up at it in bewilderment.

"Hi, my name's Lorna," I say in my best putting-people-at-ease voice. I worked as an event coordinator in my old life, and being able to read a room was as necessary as keeping a client's expectations aligned with their budget.

Her eyes dart around in a panic. Where is her family? There's always someone here to greet new Arrivals, but this girl is all alone and clearly unprepared for her death. The young usually are.

"It's okay, you're safe," I say gently, trying not to scare her.

She's dressed in jeans and a hoodie, with red Converse shoes on her feet. Her hair is a deep auburn and falls in waves past her shoulders. She looks like she should have just walked off a school bus with a backpack full of high school textbooks. I feel a pang of sorrow for whoever is expecting her to come home that day.

When she speaks, her voice is strident. "What happened? Where is he? Am I...?"

Who is supposed to be here for her? I don't know what to say. I've never been assigned as a Greeter, so I'm not sure of the routine. And it's been three years since I arrived myself.

"I'll try to answer your questions, but let's go. They'll need to use this gate for someone else."

I offer my hand and the girl takes it tentatively. Then she jerks her fingers away.

"It doesn't feel the same without a body," I explain. "But you'll get used to it."

I don't touch her again. Instead, I lead her down an avenue to a park where the trees grow tall and the grass never needs trimming. I keep the Arrival plaza in sight in case someone comes looking for the girl.

"Am I dead?" she asks, looking at her hands. Her skin is freckled and smooth, her fingers long and delicate.

"I'm afraid so." I'm not smiling now. "I guess it must have been sudden?"

The girl peers at me as if she doesn't quite see me clearly.

"I know it's hard," I say. "It was hard for me too. But there are people who can help you."

"Where am I? This doesn't look like Heaven."

I shrug. "People call it different things. I think of it as a waiting place. Some call it Limbo, but I never much cared for the Inferno."

She frowns in confusion.

"Hmm, you're probably too young for Dante. Basically, this is where we wait before passing on to whatever comes next. What most of us assume will be Heaven."

"How long do we wait?"

"That depends on you. There should have been someone to greet you when you arrived. They would be the ones to explain it all. To tell you how it works."

"Can't you tell me?" Her wide eyes remind me of a frightened animal and fill me with an overpowering urge to wrap my arms around her. She must be close to Mindi's age. It's been so long since I've felt the weight of my daughter in my arms.

I keep my hands at my sides and check over my shoulder to see if anyone from the plaza is searching for the girl. But the only people I see are waiting expectantly at the gates.

How to explain...

"Death isn't like you think. I remember when I was mortal, everyone was so afraid of dying that we did everything we could to avoid it. And if someone died... prematurely...that's all we could think about. No matter how they lived, or what they accomplished in life, if they died unexpectedly or tragically, that's all we mortals could think about. But here, none of that matters. Death is just a transition."

"Transition?" The girl jumps to her feet. "Death is no transition. It's horrible. It's a nightmare. It's..." She looks as if she's about to cry, but—as I know well—without tears it's impossible. She gasps as if trying to catch her breath, a remembered behavior from a lifetime of relying on lungs.

"I'm sorry, I've never done this before," I say apologetically, wanting to comfort her however I can. "Usually people are assigned to meet new Arrivals. For me it was my aunt. She's passed on now, but she's the one who helped me when I came. Having a familiar face made all the difference. I'm sorry that you're stuck with a stranger. And I'm sorry I'm saying it all wrong."

The girl looks at me again and her breathing calms.

"It's okay. I just..." She trails off into silence.

"Would it help to talk about it?"

She shakes her head.

"Can you at least tell me your name?"

"Jackie. Jacqueline, but I like Jackie."

I smile. "Nice to meet you, Jackie. Welcome to the afterlife."

Two

If there's only one thing I could tell you, it would be to not waste time pitying me. The living spend so much time feeling sad for people who've died because they don't realize that almost everything about our lives has gotten better.

We never get tired. Can you imagine? Nighttime only lasts a few hours here because no one needs sleep. We only have darkness because it gives us a way of marking the days and because otherwise we'd miss the stars. But it would be pointless to spend too much of our time in the dark, so we only have a few hours and then it's a new dawn with perfect colors but no morning birdsong.

We don't get hungry.

We can't feel pain.

Whatever we need—and there's very little—is provided for us. Everything about this place is comfortable. The only bad part is missing those we love, but even that isn't as non-

negotiable as you might think. I can visit old memories, such as when Dad and I got married. I love to visit that one. We were so young and had no idea what we were getting into.

I've seen both of your first days of school. I've seen you learning to ride your bikes and helping me in the kitchen and playing the piano and all those moments when I wanted time to slow down and not another day to pass.

Even better is getting to watch you in your life now. I see you making friends and crying over heartbreaks and laughing with your dad. It's not the same as being there, but it's more than you get to see of me. I wish that you could know me as I am now. I wish that you could see that I'm healthy and happy and smiling and no longer the bloated fish—

"Bloated fish?"

"Hmm?"

"You're talking about yourself, right?"

"Yeah."

"Can you explain what you mean?"

I look at Teresa, trying to figure out if she's being intentionally obtuse. Sometimes she does that just so I'll have to find the words myself. It's annoying.

"I was like a bloated fish there at the end. I don't know if it was the medication or what, but I swelled up like a balloon."

"Balloon is not 'bloated fish.'"

"It was disgusting. And I couldn't do anything about it."

"That must have been really tough. How did that make you feel?"

I gaze out the large window at the playground where children climb over a tall structure with tunnels and bridges and good old-fashioned monkey bars that almost make my palms ache with remembered blisters. There's also a giant swing set that seems to always have at least one open swing every time I look. Always room for one more. I'm glad there's a place for children to work through their transitions through play. They don't seem to stay long, passing on a lot sooner than we adults.

"I felt...hopeless. Helpless. When I looked in the mirror, I couldn't even recognize myself. It was worse than my pregnancy with Alex, and I gained eighty pounds then. But a pregnancy is something to be excited about. I would gladly put my body through that to bring a baby into the world. But cancer? It stole everything from me and I had no choice. My looks. My body. My hair. My sense of taste. My job. My dignity. My comfort. My family. My friends. I saw the pity on everyone's faces and I hated it."

"Did you ever get angry?"

"All the time," I say with a dry laugh. "And for stupid reasons. Like one time when a neighbor across the street who I didn't know very well brought over a casserole and then insisted on staying and visiting with me even though I felt like I was going to pee my pants. I needed help going to the bathroom and the whole time I was smiling and thinking, 'Why won't you just leave?' It's not her fault. She didn't know. But what really made me angry is when she told me how angelic I was, like I had chosen this or something. I didn't choose cancer! It chose me! I wanted nothing to do with it. And I didn't want her stupid casserole."

Teresa stifles a smile. "How did you express your anger?"

"How could I? I was a suffering angel, remember? So I thanked her and cried angry tears later when I was alone."

"What about Richard? Did you ever get angry with him?" Teresa watches me steadily, her dark eyes soft, yet unyielding.

I cross my legs and pull at my yoga pants to straighten the bunching under my knee. "I tried not to. He was working so hard to take care of me and the kids. Sometimes, though…"

I pause, thinking of the time that we argued over how to organize the kids' school papers. It was a small thing, a dumb thing, but I got so upset. He was the one managing the homework and the fliers and permission slips. He had a right to organize them however he wanted. But when I saw what he'd done, it felt like I was losing hold of something that I desperately didn't want to lose. It was slipping out of my grasp, and nothing I did could stop it.

When I don't continue, Teresa tries again. "I notice you always write to your kids, but it's been a while since you wrote to Richard. Why is that?"

I take a deep breath, the feeling still habitual even after three years. Why don't I write to Richard? I like Teresa well enough, but I'm not sure she's earned the answer to that question yet.

"I met someone yesterday," I say instead. "A new

Arrival. Her name is Jackie. It was strange because there wasn't anyone there to greet her."

"Is that right?" Teresa doesn't even bat an eye at the change of subject. "What did you do?"

"I tried to help her. Tried to explain where she was and why. She's young, maybe sixteen I'd guess."

"That's always tough to transition when they're so young. I'm glad you were there for her."

"I don't think I helped her all that much, though. She was having a really hard time. I was wondering if you could visit with her."

Teresa taps on her tablet, dragging her finger across the smooth surface. It reminds me of teleprompter glass from formal speaking events. Whatever she can see is lost to me. My perspective shows only her hand visible through the glass.

She makes a face. "I don't think I can take her on. I don't have time for a case like hers."

"You know about her?" I straighten with interest.

"Just looked her up. She's going to require more care than I can give her. Let me see if I can find someone..."

I wait in silence as Teresa searches.

"Hmm. I don't see anyone..."

I tap a rhythm on my armchair.

Teresa looks up apologetically. "I'm sorry, but Jackie is going to need someone special, and I just can't find... I'll keep trying. Do you mind keeping an eye on her? I'll let you know what I come up with."

I frown. "I'll do what I can, but I'm no therapist."

"Just be her friend. For now, that will be enough."

Jackie is waiting for me outside Teresa's office, leaning against the wall. She startles me so badly, I swear.

"I don't think you're supposed to curse in Heaven," she said drily.

"I told you, this isn't Heaven."

"Yeah, I figured." Jackie snorts. "Shouldn't there be, like, angels and harps and stuff? Shouldn't we all be wearing white robes?" She looks derisively over my yoga pants and t-shirt.

"I don't know anything about angels and harps, but the only people I see who wear white robes are pretentious fanatics who refuse to admit that the afterlife is nothing like they expected. That's their choice, but I like to be more comfortable."

Jackie fingers her own clothing, the same green sweatshirt I saw her in yesterday. "I don't get it. If I'm dead, why would my spirit or soul or whatever I am now be wearing my best friend's hoodie?"

I shrug, leading the way through the maze of hallways toward the lobby. "You must have liked it a lot, I guess. As near as I can tell, since nothing here is real, our environment is shaped by our own imagination. So if you imagine yourself wearing a white robe, you will. We can walk down this hallway and sit on that padded bench over there, but that's because our mortal experience tells us that we need a hallway and a bench. When I visit with Teresa in an office, I sit in a chair across a table from her because that's what my brain tells me I should do."

"Your brain?" Jackie says, one eyebrow arched doubtfully.

"Well, whatever it is that counts for a brain now."

"Super weird."

"Yeah, but also really convenient. Our imaginations fill in all the details. So I can open a door or walk on these stairs or even go climb that tree." I gesture to a brilliant red maple visible through the bank of windows that look out over the plaza. "The experience will feel remarkably real, even though none of those things exist in any form that we would consider 'real.'"

"How do you know they aren't real?"

"Because I've seen trees shift in the park, office buildings change overnight, and can even imagine into existence the furniture I want to use at any given moment."

"Is that why I was able to find you today? Because I just imagined you?"

I nod to Patsy at the front desk as we head to the outer door. She lifts her fingers in a short wave before turning back to her desk.

"Yes and no. Your need helped you find me, but I'm real enough. Dead, just like you, but real."

"So how come I can't touch you?"

"You can touch me. But it doesn't feel the way we would expect. It's more like—"

"Like fingernails on a chalkboard?"

I consider this. "Kind of, sure. It doesn't hurt, exactly. It reminds me of two notes being played side by side on the piano. You can tolerate it, but it's not very comfortable."

Outside, Reif waits on a stone bench nestled in

between two lush topiaries. He wears slim fitting corduroy pants and a soft gray pullover sweater, looking for all the world like he stepped off the cover of a men's fashion magazine. Even at my best, my imagination can't produce clothes that made me look as good as he does without even trying.

He raises his eyebrows in surprise when he sees who is with me.

"Jackie, this is my friend Reif."

He shakes her hand in the mortal way and Jackie cringes as their hands touch.

"It's like there should be something there but there isn't and so I just feel a weird buzzing or something."

"You'll get used to it. It doesn't go away, exactly, but the more you forget what real touch felt like, the less it'll bother you."

"Where do you come from, Jackie?" Reif asks.

"Seattle."

"Ha! I'm from Portland! We're neighbors!"

"Oh yeah?" Her face brightens.

"I'll warn you," Reif says, "it hardly ever rains here. I've been here six months and I think it's only rained twice."

"What do we need rain for?" I ask. "Nothing needs to grow. What's the point of getting soaked?"

"You can choose not to feel it if you don't like it," he argues.

"Yeah, but even if I don't get wet, it's still a pointless reason to endure dreary gray skies."

"What's the point of snow in the winter?" Reif challenges. "We don't need that water either."

"Because it's beautiful!"

"And so is the rain. At least to someone from the Pacific Northwest."

"You're so weird."

A smile tugs at Jackie's lips and I feel some of the gloom of my session with Teresa start to break up. It's nice to see Jackie's shell loosening. I wonder what it is about her story that made Teresa say she'll need special care.

"How was your night?" I ask her as we walk.

Her smile fades. "I don't like the dark."

"You can stay at my place tonight, if you want."

Reif chuckles. "That was such a mortal thing to say."

"What sort of place do you have?" Jackie asks.

"Same as everyone else." I point to the apartment buildings that loom in the distance on the other side of the park. "Our imaginations only take us so far here. You can't change the weather or any of the structures. I've heard rumors that if enough people need a new building or some kind of a change to the environment that it will appear."

"We should all start wishing for a Starbucks," Reif says conspiratorially.

"I was wondering about that. No food, I guess?" Jackie asks.

"Nope. Sorry."

"It's okay. It's nice not to need it. I should be starving right now, but I'm not. I like that."

"That's mature of you. It usually takes people a lot longer to realize the benefits. Reif still hasn't gotten there," I add pointedly.

Unabashed, Reif winks.

"So what is there to do here?" Jackie asks. "If we don't eat or sleep or work or go to school, what's the point? What are we supposed to do all the time?"

"There's some cool scenery," Reif says. "Canyons that are so deep they make the Grand Canyon look like a skid mark."

"I don't like heights."

"That's too bad. You can jump off a cliff here and land on your feet like nothing even happened. It's pretty cool. Not quite flying, but the closest thing I've found yet."

Jackie grimaces.

"Give her time, Reif. She's still fresh, remember?"

"Sure. There's always the Memory Bank, of course. But that's boring. Why relive something you've already had to go through once?"

But Jackie is looking at me, her brown eyes bright with interest. "What's the Memory Bank?"

"You wanna check it out? New Arrivals usually get a tour, but I'm not an authorized Greeter. I can show you how to use it, though."

In little time we're standing in front of the Memory Bank. Jackie didn't seem to notice the accelerated way we walked. Given time, she'll figure out that distance has more to do with how strong your desire to get somewhere is rather than physical proximity. It reminds me of walking on a moving walkway in an airport, only without the jarring stop.

Just inside the doors a large marble entry hall is filled with people milling around and chatting amiably. Their voices echo against the high ceiling, creating a loud murmur that always gives me a sense of satisfaction. In my mortal days, that sound was a sign that an event had achieved the right blend of relaxation and social energy. Success.

"Oh look!" Jackie touches the number that appears on the back of her hand. 1758.

"They tag you once you pass through the doors. When they call your number, you'll go to one of those elevators," I say, gesturing to the back of the room.

"You won't go with me?"

"I can go upstairs if you want, but I'm not allowed in the room when a memory is playing."

"Why not?"

"You can't intrude on someone else's memory. Unless you were there for the original, you can't visit it. But there are people there to help you. They'll explain how it works."

Reif looks around the room with agitation, his blue eyes dull in the indoor light. All trace of his typical playful humor is gone. "I'll catch you two later, all right?"

"You don't want to take a stroll down memory lane?" I ask with a smirk.

"I'd rather wear an ugly Christmas sweater. Good luck, Jackie. Don't get lost in here," he says over his shoulder as he leaves us.

"What does he mean?"

I watch Reif go with a mixture of sadness and exasperation. "He doesn't like the Memory Bank. He thinks it's a bad idea to revisit old memories. I like it. It...helps. But Reif only visits when his therapist makes him."

"He has a therapist too?"

"We all do. You'll get one soon. Some people call them Death Shrinks," I say, lowering my voice, "but that's kind of frowned on. They're really just regular people waiting here like the rest of us."

"Waiting for what?"

"For whatever comes next."

"Heaven?"

"Maybe, I don't know. But we can't get there until we've dealt with the pain of our own transitions and let it go."

"By transition you mean death?"

"Transition is a more fitting term, don't you think? I mean, do you feel dead?"

"Not exactly, though I don't have anything to compare it to." Jackie shakes her head, her ponytail swishing with the movement. "I'm not sure about seeing a therapist. Especially if they're just regular people."

"Well, they do get special training. I'm not sure how they're chosen, but there's some kind of selection process. I hear it can be tricky to be a therapist because the more you invest in the people you're helping, the harder it can be to pass on. And since that's our ultimate goal, they have certain guidelines—"

"One seven five eight."

The number sounds from a loudspeaker overhead.

"That was fast," Jackie says nervously, chewing on the drawstring of her hoodie as she searches for the bank of elevators.

"Do you want me to show you where to go?" I offer.

She shakes her head. "Nah. I can find it. Enjoy your own memory."

WHAT COMES AFTER

I watch her walk away with her shoulders hunched and her hands stuffed into her front pocket and hope the memory she's going to is a good one.

Three

Death isn't the way it looks in the movies. You know that now, and I'm sorry you had to learn it at such a young age. I'm sorry I couldn't give you a Hollywood moment where you gathered at my bedside and I sighed out my last words—wise ones, of course, that would shape the course of your life—before sinking peacefully against the pillow.

The reality is, I don't remember much about my death because I was unconscious for so much of it. When I was awake, I was so disoriented by meds or pain that sometimes I didn't even know anyone else was in the room. I've gone back since to watch my death, and it was ugly.

I'm glad your dad sent you to bed so that you didn't have to watch those last few hours as my lungs filled with fluid. But even though you didn't witness me gasping awake in a panic trying to breathe, I worry that the person lying in the bed didn't seem familiar to you anymore. That you had *already lost your mother because whatever I was, I wasn't her.*

~

The antiseptic smell of the hospital room washes over me almost before any other sense. A large window bathes the room in a pale light, rendering the cream-colored walls, white sheets, and laminate floor an image of stale cleanliness.

I look at myself resting in the bed and can almost feel the pressure on my hips and tailbone from sitting there hour after hour. I'm alone, my head leaning on a pillow. I'm staring out the window at the parking lot with a serious expression on my face.

I've seen this memory so many times that I'm no longer uncomfortable watching this private moment when my fears are etched in the lines around my mouth and eyes. Alone with my thoughts, my expression is unguarded. Naked.

I can see it all. The pain. The fear. The worry about the future. The uncertainty and anger.

I move closer to the hospital bed and reach out to touch the blanket. But this is only a memory, so I feel nothing.

"I'm so sorry," I tell the me sitting in the bed. "It's going to get so much harder. I wish I could say that the surgery is going to work and you're going to be fine. But it's not. There are some days that you're going to wish you were dead. And then you're going to die and wish more than anything you could go back in time and be alive again. But I promise that as scary as it is right now, when the worst happens, it won't be so bad. You'll be so amazed at how much better you feel. You'll make friends on the other side, and you'll get to see Mindi and Alex grow up. Richard will make it through and be a better single dad than you think. They'll be okay. And you'll be okay, too."

The me sitting in the bed can't hear me. I'm not really there.

But I swear I almost feel the breeze when the door opens. And I almost smell the brownies Mindi brings in on a platter, their flaky crust practically making my mouth water.

"Happy Birthday!" Mindi cries, her bright green eyes sparkling with the joke.

Alex bounds into the room after her, already tall and lanky for his ten years. He holds a large grouping of mylar balloons in black reading "Over the Hill" and "Happy Birthday."

The version of me in the bed grins, packing away the emotions from before in a heartbeat. "What is this?" I ask.

Richard comes in last with a bouquet of red roses and a sheepish grin.

"Happy Birthday," he says, bending to kiss me as he hands me the bouquet. He's shaved and dressed in clean clothes. By comparison, I look like a creature out of a horror film with my blotchy skin and lank hair and institutional gown. But I've watched this memory enough to truly see how he looks at me, and I know he doesn't see the facial hair that needs plucking or the gray emerging in my roots. It still fills me with wonder that he can look at me as if I'm still the beauty he married sixteen years earlier.

"It's not my birthday!" I say with a laugh.

"This is a pre-birthday party," Mindi says, plopping the plate of brownies in my lap and offering me a hug. I return it awkwardly, mindful of the IV tubes pulling my arm.

"We're just practicing," Alex says, climbing up to sit at the foot of my bed. "Trying to get you used to the idea of turning forty."

"But I'm only thirty-eight!" I protest.

"It'll be here before you know it," Richard says ominously. In my mind, I recite the line with him.

And so it goes. Mindi tells me all about her eighth grade band concert and Alex asks if he can have an ice cream from the cafeteria before they leave. I have all the dialogue memorized and cringe when I ignore Richard's attempt to tell me a story about a coworker because Mindi interrupts with a question about whether I'll be out of the hospital in time for Halloween. I forgot to go back and ask Richard to share his story, and to this day I still don't know what it was he wanted to tell me.

When the memory ends and fades to black, I let out a sigh.

"We hope you enjoyed your memory," a polite recorded voice says. "If you would like to watch another, please make your request with the Memory Facilitator assigned to you."

The Memory room has black walls, floor, and ceiling, but light emanates from some indirect source, and I can see my reflection clearly in the dark surface. The face that looks back at me now is healthy and young without a wrinkle or a hint of gray in my walnut-colored hair. This is the me I remember, not that sickly creature in the hospital bed. I think about the white-haired woman I watched arrive the day before and wonder if I looked this vibrant when I first transitioned or if I resembled how I looked when I died. I should ask Reif if he thinks I've changed in the time he's known me.

A Memory Facilitator waits outside the door to escort me downstairs.

"I have a friend named Jackie in room 1758. Can you tell me if she's finished?" I ask him.

He taps the tablet in his hand. "She has two minutes and nineteen seconds left in her memory."

Good. I'd hoped to finish before her so I could be there when she gets out. The first time can be a little unsettling. I've known people to plunge into despair with the fresh reminder of what they've lost, or binge-watch obsessively for hours. Jackie is so young, I worry that she won't know how to stop.

I wait for Jackie in the lobby, sitting in a padded chair near the elevators. The longer I wait, the more concerned I get. I hope she chose well. Not just a happy memory, but one that will give her a sense of satisfaction or completion rather than business left unfinished. The Memory Facilitators are good about making recommendations if you aren't sure what you want to see, but a proper Greeter would have guided her so much better than I have.

When the elevator doors open, Jackie stumbles out

with her hand over her mouth and a look of panic on her face. She bolts for the outer door without noticing me.

I curse under my breath and run after her, pushing through the crowd gathered in the lobby. When I step out into the sunlight, I barely glimpse her disappearing into the wooded park.

"Jackie!" I call, but she doesn't look back.

I run down the steps and follow. Although she has a head start, I know I'll easily catch her. It's the same reason she found me earlier today just by thinking of me. Getting anywhere in this world is less about distance and more about desire. I can cover a far greater distance than she can because I want to catch her. But Jackie isn't running *to* anything.

I can't remember the last time I ran like this. Running holds no appeal for me in this world. Sure, I don't get winded and can literally run forever. But I miss the feel of my muscles stretching and working, my heart pounding, and that happy exhaustion that comes from a good run. This is just...going. There's no effort and no reward.

If Jackie notices the difference, it doesn't change her stride. She runs through the woods as if she'll never stop. I catch up to her just as she reaches a wooden bridge spanning a creek that looks like something out of a postcard. Fallen leaves carpet the shore and white foam highlights rocks as water spills over them.

Jackie stops in the middle of the bridge and grasps the railing, doubling over as if in pain. She heaves desperately as if she wants to vomit but can't.

"Are you okay?" I ask as I approach, cautious of her suffering. "I should have warned you what sort of memory to choose for your first time. It's usually better to start with something that doesn't have too much strong emotion."

She doesn't answer, just lets out a choked sob and a moan.

"Do you want to talk about it?"

Jackie's eyes are wide and pleading. "I can't..."

"It's all right. Not until you're ready. We have all the time in the world."

I stand next to her, wishing I could pull her to me. Wondering if she wants me to try.

After a few minutes, she calms and we stand in silence, side by side, watching the water run over the rocks and under our feet. If only I could comfort her the way I would have comforted my own kids. Instead, I stand as close as I dare and hope just being there will help her not feel so alone.

Four

"Jackie needs help," I tell Reif that night as we sit on my balcony watching the stars come out after a glorious sunset.

"Yeah she does. What are they teaching high schoolers these days? Imagine thinking Steinbeck is a guitar manufacturer."

"That's not what I mean. She's really struggling with her transition. She won't talk about her family or how she died or any of the things new Arrivals normally like to talk about. I think it must have been really tragic."

"She's a teenager. Of course it was tragic."

Pinpricks of light emerge in a pale sky tending toward dark, and I put on a soft sweater in peachy tones without thinking, vaguely realizing it's the color of the sunset we were watching earlier.

"I assumed it was a car accident or something, but do you think maybe she could have died by suicide? I don't want to ask, but I can't help but wonder."

"If that's the case, she's going to need a little more than your average therapy."

"Teresa said she'd look into finding someone good. I hope she gets help soon."

Reif leans back in his chair and stretches his long legs out, propping his feet on the edge of a planter. "It's too bad. She seems like a good kid. Not really your troubled type."

"Maybe I'm reading too much into it." I look through the glass door to my room where Jackie lays on the couch looking up at the ceiling. Every light in the room is on. I showed her how to adjust the lights by imagining the room dimmer or brighter, thinking that would help her learn how to interact with this world a little better. But she just turned them as bright as they would go and left them there.

When I look back at Reif, he's watching me with a half smile. "You must have been a good mom."

"Why do you say that?"

"Look at you. Worrying over Jackie, trying to take care of her."

"Is that so weird?"

"No, not weird at all. It's kind of cute, actually. Like your mom genes have gone into hyperactive mode now that someone needs you."

"I don't know about that." If I were mortal, I would be blushing. Just what does he mean by that? And why does it feel like he's laughing at me?

I decide to change the subject.

"How'd your therapy go today?"

Reif shrugs. "How does it ever go?"

"Meaningful and full of healing connections?"

He snorts. "Yeah, right."

"If you'd actually talk to Winston about what's holding you back, he might be able to help."

"Says the woman who's been here for three years and still can't let go."

"That's not fair!" I object. "Teresa tells me that with some people it takes longer. The happier they were in life, the harder it is to let go of what they lost."

"Maybe." Reif says noncommittally.

"What's that supposed to mean?" I look at him sharply. Something about his tone sounds off.

The familiar twinkle in his blue eyes is gone. "I just wonder sometimes if your perfect family was really as perfect as you say. Maybe one of the reasons you're struggling to let go is because you can't see your life for what it really was."

I open my mouth but the words won't come. Where did that come from? It's not like Reif to be so negative. That's one of the reasons I like having him around.

"What do you know about it?" I sputter. "Just because you didn't have a loving family doesn't mean that *my* family life was dysfunctional."

"I'm not suggesting it was dysfunctional, Lorna. But no one's kids are that angelic. No one's marriage is that perfect. I would believe it a little more if you had bad things to say once in a while. I wonder sometimes if the person you're most trying to convince is yourself."

"Wow. Would it make you feel better if I said I was as miserable as you? Is that what you want?"

Reif frowns. "You hear yourself? Sounds pretty

defensive to me. If your life was all that great, why would you need to be defensive?"

"I can't believe you right now!" My voice cracks a little. Anger isn't something I'm used to feeling here in this world where there's so little conflict. With great effort, I try to lower my voice and speak calmly. "I don't know what sort of issues you've got, but it's not fair to take them out on me. Of course my life wasn't perfect. I wasn't perfect, my kids weren't perfect. Richard wasn't perfect. But it was the closest thing to perfection I've ever known, and I'd go back to it in a second."

"Yeah, but that's the point. You can't go back! And the sooner you can accept that, the better."

"What is your deal, Reif? Are you jealous? Is that it? Just because you were a miserable drunk who wasted his life doesn't mean that you should begrudge me my happiness."

Reif stands, rocking the planter with a dull thud. "You know what, I don't have to listen to this. See you later." Rather than going back through the apartment, he climbs over the railing and drops over the edge.

It gives me a jolt of panic to see him fall like that, even though I know he'll land safely. I still have to look over the edge of the railing to make sure he's okay.

He doesn't look up as he stalks away into the night.

What is his problem? I review our conversation and try to figure out how I upset him. Was it asking about counseling? For all his good humor and friendliness, Reif is very private. It took me almost four months to find out how he died. He swore it was an accident, but now I wonder. Maybe there's more to his story than I know. Maybe talking about Jackie is too upsetting for him.

But that doesn't give him the right to be so rude about my life. It's not like I did anything wrong. I died of cancer, for crying out loud.

I go back inside. My room is a single room for a single person, like all the rooms in every apartment building in this place. No need for kitchens or bathrooms or bedrooms or laundry rooms. Just a private place where I can spend time alone writing letters to my kids that are never sent. Mine is decorated with rugs and large pillows and overstuffed bean bags, as if I'm waiting for guests to come and hang out. But usually it's just me. And sometimes Reif.

Jackie sits up as I walk in and slides over to make room for me on the couch.

"It's weird not to be able to sleep," she says. "I can't decide if I like it or not."

"I think it's pretty great. In my old life, I never got enough sleep."

"Me neither. But still, it seems pretty boring, Nothing really to do. Doesn't it get old?"

"There's plenty to do. You'll see when you start therapy. Not only will you meet with your counselor, you'll have assignments for things to do in between."

"Assignments?" Jackie grimaces.

"Stuff to help work through whatever pain you brought with you from your transition."

"I don't want to do therapy. I just want people to leave me alone."

"Now that *would* be boring," I say with a smile.

Jackie is silent for a moment. "Where's Reif?"

"He went home."

"So is he like your boyfriend or something?"

"What? No!" Again that feeling like I should be blushing. "He's just a friend. I'm married!"

Jackie smirks, her nose wrinkling. "You mean that 'till death do you part' thing?"

I must still feel defensive from my conversation with Reif, because I speak more hotly than I intend. "I love Richard. He's still my husband. I don't care what the pastor said, we're still married."

"Cool. Whatever." Jackie pushes herself to her feet and goes outside to look at the stars, leaving me alone with my indignation.

Five

The permanence of death is one of the hardest things to get used to. Since I still feel like myself, it's hard to remember that there's no going back. That this isn't just a surreal dream and someday I'll wake up. But the more I see visions of you in your life now—your life without me—the more the permanence of death settles in.

Without me, you are both growing into different people than you would have been if I'd lived. It's not a bad thing, necessarily. I'm proud of how compassionate and thoughtful you are. But your lives are forever changed because I'm not there.

I'm here instead. I live on. Death may be just a transition, but it only goes one way. There really is no going back.

∼

"I haven't been able to find anyone who can take Jackie," Teresa tells me when I meet with her the next day.

"Uh..." I stare at her like I'm waiting for the punchline. It feels like I'm explaining the obvious and I try not to show my annoyance. "She really needs help. How can there not be anyone?"

"Sometimes cases like hers take a while to find the right person."

"So what am I supposed to do with her?"

Teresa draws back, her finger paused above her tablet. "You sound resentful. I thought you were happy to help. But if she's become a burden or an inconvenience—"

"No, it's not that. It's just that she really needs help, and I'm not trained to give it to her. I feel like I'm letting her down," I say with exasperation.

"Does she seem disappointed in you?"

"No, but it's not like she has anyone else to compare me to. I can't understand why no one was there to greet her. I've never seen that before."

"I've seen it," Teresa says. "Not frequently, but every so often. It manages to work out one way or another."

Her nebulous answer isn't very comforting. Through the window I watch the children playing outside on the playground. They seem so carefree and unburdened. They surely had hard lives to die so young, but you wouldn't guess it to see them laughing and chasing each other. I wish Jackie could shed her pain so easily.

"So what should I do with her?" I ask. "She doesn't want to talk about how she died. I think she's ashamed. What do I do about that?"

"If you were ashamed about something, how would you want someone else to approach it?"

I consider this. "I suppose I wouldn't want them to talk about it at all. But that's not necessarily for the best, is it?"

"So if they *had* to ask you about it, what would you want them to say?"

~

"Jackie, do you wanna see a vision?"

"A vision?" Jackie looks up from where she's relacing her sneakers for the third time, trying to make both sides perfectly even. "Sounds like some weird religious crap."

"No, nothing like that." I grin and sit next to her on the smooth wooden bench. "Just like you can go back and visit memories from your life, you can also watch current visions of the people you care about. See what they're doing right now this moment."

Jackie's hands still. "I can see my mom?"

"Absolutely."

She hastily finishes tying her sneaker and stands. Her hair is tied back in a ponytail and little wisps frame her face like a halo.

"I'll warn you, it's a little different than memories," I explain. "A memory is a projection of your experience. A vision is an experience you haven't had. It's not your story, so there are a lot more restrictions to it. You're limited to only thirty minutes per week, and can only view people you've had a close connection to. On the plus side, I can come with you if you want because there's no risk of interfering."

"Nah, that's okay," Jackie says. "So, how do I see one of these?"

"We'll go to the Station. It's kind of like a huge train station, but each car is individual and takes you to a specific location. Rather than the memory being recreated in a special room for you, you have to actually go to the vision."

"Cool. Let's go."

Instead of leaving Jackie with instructions and hoping for the best this time, I accompany her to talk to the Vision Coordinator behind the counter.

"I want to see my mom," Jackie says firmly.

The Coordinator looks at Jackie and swipes her screen. "Let me just make sure this isn't a violation—"

"A violation of what?" Jackie asks indignantly. "She's my mom!"

The woman smiles patiently, showing a slight gap between her front teeth. "We respect the living's privacy. No visiting during times of particular vulnerability. Bathroom or bedroom routines, that sort of thing."

"Ah." Jackie nods. "That makes sense."

"Looks like your mom is...let's see. It looks like she's at the police station." She shoots Jackie a wary glance. "Do you want to visit another time?"

"No, that's fine."

Police station? That doesn't sound good. I remember her reaction to the Memory Bank and my suspicions about taking her own life.

"Are you sure you don't want me to come with you? It can be a bit unnerving your first time." *Even without a visit to the police station.*

Jackie looks at me, and her eyes flicker with apprehension. "Yeah, I guess. It might be a good idea."

We pass through the gate onto the platform. Jackie fidgets nervously with the string of her hoodie.

"You know, you can change your clothes any time you want," I say.

Jackie looks down. "I like what I'm wearing."

When the car comes for us, she steps back uncertainly. It moves faster than any subway or light rail I knew in life, but without the vibration that announces its arrival.

The door slides open. "Vision for Jackie Renfro," a recorded voice announces.

Jackie hesitates only a moment, glancing back at me. I smile reassuringly, hiding the unease I felt. Together, we step aboard.

The door slides shut and the speaker announces, "Please be aware that you have thirty minutes remaining in this week's vision allotment. If at any time you choose to abort this vision, simply return to the car. The unused time will be credited toward another vision of your choice."

There is no sensation of movement from within the car, but lights and shapes flashing past outside make it clear we're moving. Within only a few short moments, the lights still and the voice announces, "Arrived."

We step out of the car and into an office with a low ceiling and fluorescent lights. A plaque on the wall and the nameplate on the desk indicates this is the police chief's office. A potted plant fills one corner, but it doesn't quite succeed in making the industrial carpet and walls made of concrete blocks look inviting. I lean forward to see if the plant is real or not. The leaves are frayed, their individual threads showing. Fake, then.

A red-haired woman in a tailored jacket and ankle boots sits in front of a desk. She's texting on a phone with a sleek silver case.

"Mom!" Jackie cries. She reaches out a hand and then stops abruptly, looking at her arm. Her skin shimmers translucently.

"This isn't a memory," I explain. "This is real. Happening right now. But we don't exist in this world, so anything you say or do has no impact on what's going on."

Jackie moves forward anyway and tries to put her hand on her mom's shoulder. It slides right through.

Her mom's expression doesn't change. She continues texting, her thumbs moving furiously.

"I'm sorry to keep you waiting, Mrs. Renfro."

Jackie's mother stands as the police chief enters the room. The chief wears a deep blue blouse and gray dress pants and reaches forward awkwardly to shake hands, a thick file pinned under her arm. She looks like she should be standing in front of a classroom.

Her eyes are keen and sad. "I really wish I had better news, but as I said on the phone, we think that we've found your daughter. This is never the outcome we want in a situation like this."

Mrs. Renfro nods. "Of course."

"My detectives are still at the scene. But they sent me a picture if you're willing to do a preliminary identification."

"You mean she isn't here?" Mrs. Renfro's voice cracks and she swallows.

"Yes, I am, Mom," Jackie whispers. "I'm right here."

"Not yet," the chief answers simultaneously. "In cases like this, we want to be very thorough. I don't anticipate that we'll bring her body in for a few hours at least."

"I want to see her."

The chief nods and opens the file, withdrawing three sheets of paper. Printouts of digital photos.

I can't see them well and really don't care to. But Jackie moves forward to get a better look, peering at the photos in her mom's hands.

Mrs. Renfro's hand trembles. "My baby girl."

The chief nods. "This is Jackie, then?"

"Where did you find her?"

"A trucker found her in a dumpster at a rest stop a few miles out of town."

I start. A dumpster?

Mrs. Renfro lets out a choked sob.

I look at Jackie. Even though I can scarcely make out the outline of her features, her expression looks fierce.

"Do you know what happened? Who did this to her?" Mrs. Renfro asks, sinking back into her chair.

The chief sits next to her. "Not yet. Her phone wasn't with her, but we're scouring the area to search for it. We're also looking through CCTV and interviewing everyone who saw her the day she disappeared. We're putting every resource available into pursuing every lead. But you have to understand, a homicide investigation like this is very complex."

"I told them!" Mrs. Renfro says. "I told those detectives she didn't run away!"

"I understand this is very upsetting. Our detectives have to consider every possibility, but I assure you that they've dedicated every waking moment to finding your daughter," the chief says. "We're doing everything we can to—"

Before the chief finishes her sentence, Jackie turns on her heel and runs back to the car.

"Jackie, hold on!" I trot after her, jumping in the car just before the door slides closed.

"You have fourteen minutes remaining in this vision," the cool voice announces. "You may apply these minutes to another vision when you return to the Station.

Inside the car, Jackie's form has returned to normal. Her face is pinched as if she wants to cry.

Words jam in my throat. What can I say? "I'm so sorry, Jackie," I manage weakly. "I didn't know."

She's quiet for a long time, watching the flashing lights and vague color on the other side of the glass. When she finally speaks, her voice is tight.

"Did you see those pictures?"

"No."

"He left me naked. Naked! Why couldn't he have left my clothes on? It's bad enough what he did to me, but did he have to leave me naked for my mother to see! Now she has to think of me like that."

"Who did that to you?" I think of how little the chief seemed to know. It's frustrating that Jackie can't just talk to her and tell her everything that happened.

Jackie meets my gaze, but her eyes don't focus properly. "I don't know. I never saw his face." She shudders and turns back to the window.

No wonder she doesn't like the dark.

Six

Reif answers his door wearing a t-shirt and flannel pajama pants. I can't help it. I laugh.

He looks down and shrugs. "Old habits die hard."

"I don't think I've ever seen you in anything more casual than a J. Crew button-up and tailored slacks."

"J. Crew?" He thumped his chest. "I'm wounded. And Mario's would be scandalized. Besides, I do wear jeans sometimes."

"Do you?"

"Not all of us think workout clothes are the epitome of fashion."

"They're comfy. What can I say?"

"Ditto," he says, gesturing to his pajama pants.

"Are you going to invite me in? Or do we have to have this conversation in the hallway?"

Reif stands aside so I can pass. His room looks the same as mine, though his is more sparsely furnished. A couch, a table with a single chair, and a bookshelf with a lava lamp on top are the only notable objects.

Despite knowing these things don't exist in our world, seeing him in pajamas still makes me half expect to see empty liquor bottles or other signs of a bender. Ordinarily I would make a joke about it, but I don't dare considering how our last conversation ended.

"I'm sorry I upset you yesterday," I begin.

He waves my apology away. "Don't worry about it. What's up?"

I sink onto the couch and make a show of fluffing a throw pillow to hide my disappointment. Reif and I argue all the time, but never for real. I want to understand what I said wrong. For him to dismiss the topic feels like he doesn't trust me. And considering that he has yet to offer me a real smile, I know he isn't over it yet.

But he clearly doesn't want to talk about it, so I change the subject.

"I learned how Jackie died."

"Oh yeah?"

"It was pretty awful. She was murdered." It feels weird to say the words so casually.

"No kidding?" He looks at me with the first sign of interest he's shown since opening his door.

"She doesn't know who did it. Sounds like the police don't have many leads. I feel so bad for her."

He shakes his head. "That's rough. Where is she now?"

"My room. I don't know what to do for her. Teresa says she can't find anyone to take her on. Apparently there's a bit of a wait."

"You'd think a case like hers would get higher priority."

"Right? It's really frustrating." I expect some sort of clever quip, but he just looks at me. "You okay, Reif?"

"Sure."

"You don't seem...yourself."

"I'm fine. I just have a lot on my mind."

"You wanna talk about it?"

"Trust me, it's nothing you'd want to hear," he scoffs, running a hand through his fair hair and down his jaw.

I feel a twinge of...something. Pain? Jealousy? I share everything with him, so it hurts to be reminded of how much he keeps from me.

He must have read the expression on my face and regretted his words because his voice is gentler when he speaks again. "Don't worry about me. I just needed to get my brooding on. It'll pass. So, what are you going to do about Jackie?"

"I think first I need to make sure she feels safe. Be there for her if she wants to talk, but don't pressure her if she doesn't. It broke my heart to see her mom there at the police station. Can you imagine losing someone like that?"

"Only in my worst nightmares."

"So, what do you think?"

"About what?"

"My idea? Do you think that's a good approach?"

Reif smiles and his eyes glint. It's a hint of the old Reif and makes me feel more settled than I have all day. "You came here to ask me for advice?"

"Of course! You're my best friend. Who else would I ask?"

"You've been here three years. I've been here six months. Neither one of us can get our own crap together. What makes you think we can help this girl?"

"I don't know, but it's worth trying. She doesn't have anyone else. And come on, what else have we got to do?"

"Me?" Reif says mockingly. "You wouldn't believe how full my schedule is. In fact, I'm late for a coffee date." His clothes instantly change to a dress suit.

I roll my eyes but can't suppress a snicker. "Whatever. Thanks for nothing, Reif."

"Anytime." He pulls the door wide and bows as I leave.

"Such a nerd," I mutter under my breath.

"And that's why you love me," he responds with a wink.

My smile falters, suddenly reminded of Jackie's question about whether he's my boyfriend. Of course he's just kidding, but it still makes me feel...like I'm doing something illicit.

When I get back to my room, Jackie is lying on the couch, looking up at the ceiling. The lights are cycling from dim to bright and back again like some super surge brownout.

"Guess you figured out how to use the lights?"

Jackie grunts.

"I was thinking, what would you say to going to see Teresa with me tomorrow?"

Jackie glances at me. "Who's Teresa? Your shrink?"

"My counselor, yeah."

"Uh, no. No way."

"You sure? She's really nice. Maybe if you talk to her yourself she'll be able to get you in to see someone sooner."

"I don't want to see someone at all."

"It might be good if you talked about it."

Jackie stands up abruptly and walks to the balcony. "You don't get it. I don't want to talk to anyone about it."

I sigh. The lights stop pulsing as soon as Jackie leaves the room.

I can't blame her for not wanting to share. I saw my own viewing and was so uncomfortable looking at my corpse lying there like some grotesque wax figure that I almost didn't bother going to the funeral. As hard as the process was for me, how much worse would it have been if I'd died the way Jackie did?

"All right," Jackie says, poking her head back in the room. "I'll talk to someone on one condition."

"What's that?"

"If they'll help me figure out who did it."

I hesitate. "I'm not sure that fits their mission. The point is to learn to let go of the trauma of death—"

"Then forget it." She disappears back outside.

I join her on the balcony and look out over the city of similar buildings broken up by parks and wild areas. Mountains loom in the distance, but I've never visited them to see if they are real or just window dressing.

"Do you think finding out who did it will help you let go?" I ask.

"Maybe," Jackie says. "The way I feel right now, I

don't know if I'll ever be able to let go. But that would be a good place to start."

I idly pluck at a trumpeter vine climbing a trellis against the wall. "Let me see what I can find out. Maybe they'll allow it if it's necessary to helping you pass on."

Jackie nods once. "But not Teresa."

"Why?"

"How good can she be? You've been seeing her for three years and still haven't learned to let go yourself."

I don't answer. I've only been seeing Teresa for four months, having been through seven therapists before her. But I don't correct Jackie. Her details might be off, but she's still painfully right.

Seven

Weirdly, it doesn't hurt. So much of those final days I barely remember, but I do remember being afraid of what would come after I died. Not Heaven and Hell; I'd never been very religious. My biggest fear was that it would hurt.

It didn't.

In fact, it was just the opposite.

As I left my body, the constant pain fell away and was replaced instead with the most amazing feeling of energy and power and...freedom. I could move in ways I hadn't in years. I left my weak, broken, sick body behind and stepped into this world where I never feel pain or exhaustion or hunger ever again.

You'd think I would have never wanted to look back.

Then why can't I seem to move forward?

"What comes next? After we pass on?"

Teresa offers a half smile. "You know I can't answer that. I'm here just like you."

"Yeah, but do you get special instruction about it as a therapist? How do you know it's worth helping all these people pass on if you don't even know what that means? Surely they give you some idea of what to expect."

Teresa leans her elbows on the table and clasps her hands together. "If I knew, don't you think I would tell you? We would tell everyone."

"Haven't you ever wondered why it's all such a secret?" I ask, uncrossing my legs and leaning forward. "If it's so great, why not let us all know what to expect? Why all the secrecy? If I hadn't seen people pass on myself, I would start to wonder if it's a hoax. Maybe you're all part of some big conspiracy."

I'm feeling tetchy today. It's not Teresa's fault, but she started our session telling me that there still isn't anyone available to take Jackie's case, and I'm looking for someone to blame.

Teresa is too experienced to take my bait. "That's for you to decide, I guess. Certainly you aren't the first one to wonder if it's worth it. I can't tell you how many people I've known personally who have given up therapy, choosing instead to stay for years shadowing their loved ones in Visions or reliving their greatest hits in the Memory Bank."

"Maybe that's what I should do, too," I say, though the thought makes me queasy. "Reif thinks I spend too much time there as it is."

Teresa smiles at my mention of Reif. "Reif is quite the

paradox, isn't he? He avoids both Memories and Visions, and yet he still hasn't passed on."

"What do you know about Reif?" I ask, surprised.

"Winston and I talk."

"That seems...inappropriate. Whatever happened to patient-client privilege?"

"This isn't mortality. Of course we aim to be discreet, but it's frequently helpful to consult with therapists of family members."

"Reif isn't family."

"Close friends, then. Whether you realize it or not, Reif's friendship has helped you more than you know." She reaches for her tablet and scans the screen. "Since meeting Reif, you've spent less time on either Memories or Visions and more time wrestling with those difficult questions that will ultimately help you to let go."

"Such as?"

"Is it worth it? That's an important one right there."

"I don't know. That sounds pretty skeptical to me."

"Sure. But that means you're also open to the possibility that the answer may be 'yes.'"

The Memory Facilitator towers over Jackie and me. If he wasn't an NBA all-star in mortality, he missed his true calling.

"I'm sorry, that won't be possible," he says.

"Why not?" Jackie asks with one hand on a cocked hip and a heaping dose of attitude. "If I say that she can come in and visit a memory with me, why isn't that allowed?"

"We do it for your own protection," the man says patiently. He's wearing a gray three-piece suit, the tablet dwarfed by his gigantic hands. "Memories are malleable things. When you visit a memory, you aren't going to a specific place in space and time. You're simply experiencing a recreation we have engineered for you here in this room, based on the data we retrieve from your memory. However, our memories can be easily influenced. If we introduce a new person into this room, it might color your perception and alter your experience. Our goal is to keep your memories as pure as possible."

Jackie frowns at me. "I guess I'll have to visit it by myself, then."

"Are you sure about that?" I ask, thinking of the panic her first memory induced.

"I'll just visit the theater. See what I can come up with."

I nod uncertainly and leave Jackie to the memory of her abduction.

But as soon as I leave the room, I'm surprised to meet Reif hurrying down the hall toward me.

"Sorry I'm late," he says in a breathless tone, a carry-over from mortality. We all do it, mimicking sounds and habits tied to breathing even though we no longer use lungs.

"What are you—" I can't finish before he pushes through the door and into the room where Jackie waits with the Memory Facilitator.

"Jackie! Sorry to keep you waiting," he says cheerfully as the door closes behind him.

Stunned, I hurry after him in time to see him slip a card to the facilitator.

"Lorna can stay too." He nods at me.

The facilitator swipes the card. "Very well, Winston. Welcome back, Lorna."

Winston?

I stare at Reif. His eyes twinkle but he doesn't crack a smile. I don't dare speak until the Memory Facilitator leaves the room. Jackie watches him go with a ghost of a smile.

"What did you do?" she whispers to Reif. "Who's Winston?"

"Never mind that," he says. "Do you mind if I join you? I'm afraid Lorna wouldn't make a very convincing Winston."

He nudges me playfully, and I step away from the dissonant hum between us. At least he seems to have thrown off his earlier gloom.

"You wanna help me?" Jackie asks.

"Of course. Why wouldn't I?"

Jackie shrugs. "All right."

I tuck away my questions for later.

The room whirs softly and the walls disappear as the image of a parking lot appears around us. A sprawling plaza spans the distance, but the street lamps lighting the empty parking stalls are dim. Only a few cars sit clustered near the plaza entrance.

"All right, Jackie," Reif says. "Tell us as much as you can about what we're seeing here."

"Um, this is the movie theater?"

"Okay. What day is it? What time? Why are you here? Who are you with? Who knew you would be there?"

"Reif?" I say, surprised at the rapid questions.

"Hey, we've gotta know what she was doing and why. You never know what's going to be important."

"I was just meeting friends," Jackie says.

"Do you have a car?"

"No. I only live a couple of blocks away." She points to the far end of the parking lot. Sure enough, a figure in a gray peacoat is walking toward us from a brightly lit intersection.

"It seems awfully late to be here alone," Reif observes. "Looks like the theater is about to close, if it hasn't already."

"What are you, my dad?" Jackie snaps.

"It's okay," I say soothingly, shooting a dark look at Reif. "Whatever happened here wasn't your fault. But it would be good to know what was going on."

Jackie looks away. "I was just meeting a couple of friends. They'd been to a late movie and texted me to see if I wanted to go out and get something to eat."

"Who are they? What are their names?"

Jackie glares at Reif. "What is this? Why are you grilling me?"

"Because you're a teenager out late on a school night acting like you're guilty."

"Reif!" I protest.

Jackie tries to hold his gaze, but can't. She hangs her head sheepishly. "My mom didn't know. She thought I was doing homework. I had a big test in Math the next day and was supposed to be studying. But Vince and Ray texted and I wanted a break."

"Guy friends?"

"Ray's a girl. Short for Raylene. They're chill, I swear."

She stops talking because the memory version of her is approaching. She strides down the sidewalk confidently, her red hair tucked under a slouchy beanie, and boots clicking in rhythm on the concrete.

"Pause memory," Reif commands.

Memory Jackie stops mid-stride.

Reif turns and peers into the darkness at the edges of the memory. I follow his gaze, but can't see anything except dumpsters, buildings, and cookie-cutter plantings that blur out the further away they get from Jackie. It's a typical memory distortion. Familiar places are filled in with general awareness but not specific details because in that moment she wasn't paying close attention.

I move closer to Memory Jackie, cringing at the hopeful expression on her face. Knowing what's coming.

"Did anyone else know you were coming here tonight?" Reif's voice is grave.

Jackie shakes her head. She, too, stares at her memory self. "The police wouldn't even know where to look. Mom probably didn't notice I was missing until the next morning."

"Do you have any siblings? Anyone else live with you?"

Jackie shakes her head once.

"You ready to continue?"

She nods.

"Play memory."

I feel as if I'm holding my breath, dread clawing at my middle over what I know is coming.

Memory Jackie resumes walking, skipping forward a little as she rounds the corner of the big, squat building and the theater comes into view.

I move desperately, scanning the area and wondering if her killer is already approaching. If she didn't see him that night, neither will we.

The headlights of a car pass over her and away as a vehicle turns toward the exit of the lot. Memory Jackie swivels in response, distracted momentarily. When she looks back toward the theater, everything changes.

The memory flickers and fades at the same time that Memory Jackie grunts.

"Oh! Excuse me—Ow! Stop! Let go—"

The rest of her words are stifled. She tries to scream but something muffles her voice. All around us is dark and we stand frozen in the empty room, listening to the sounds of her being carried away—boots scuffling against concrete and a man's labored breathing close by.

Jackie stares into nothingness, her eyes wide. Reif's eyes are shadowed, and I can't tell what he's thinking. I feel an urge to reach out and grasp them both, but I hold still, feeling the physical separation keenly.

"This memory does not have enough information to continue," a cool voice sounds overhead. "We hope you enjoyed your memory and apologize for the malfunction."

The dim lights come on again, reflecting in the black surfaces of the walls and floor.

I struggle to find my voice. "Jackie?"

She looks right through me.

"Jackie, are you okay?"

"I want to find him," she says hoarsely. "I *will* find him. And then I'll kill him."

Eight

We don't call ourselves ghosts. Ghosts are something out of children's tales or scary movies or Halloween. We're just people, like we were in mortality. Moms and dads and teachers and store clerks and postal carriers and truck drivers. I don't know where the idea of ghosts came from, but I wonder sometimes if after you pass on you get a little more freedom to interact with the mortal world. Some people I've met here think so.

I still don't believe in traditional ghosts, though. Not the scary ones that come to torment us for disturbing their sleep or in payment for our sins. But loved ones who've passed on coming and giving the occasional boost? Sure, why not?

That's what I would do.

I miss hot chocolate. For all Reif's obsessed with coffee, I don't miss it at all. But hot chocolate is another story.

That was the best way to end a cold, snowy day or settle disappointment from a failure—hands wrapped around a steaming mug filled with thick sweetness. That's what I would have fixed for Jackie when we returned to my room.

But my hands are empty as I close the glass door and step out onto the balcony where Reif sits in a wicker chair.

He tosses me a soft throw and I wrap it around my shoulders as I settle into the empty chair next to him, seeking comfort from the familiar feeling of shielding myself from the world with a cozy blanket.

"So...Winston?"

Reif's grim expression softens. "Worked pretty well, didn't it?"

"Yeah, but how? You don't look anything like Winston. Did you smuggle a black market ID-maker when you transitioned or something?"

"Yeah." His lips twitch in a smile. "Right next to my money printer."

"I didn't think that kind of deceit was possible here."

Reif shrugs. He's never told me what he did for a living when he was alive. The way he dresses, I've always assumed he was a professional of some kind. Consultant or businessman or salesman. But suddenly I imagine him in a very different line of work. Something dishonest. Even sinister.

"How's she doing?" Reif asks, pulling my thoughts away from images of him as an assassin for hire or working for a drug cartel.

I glance through the door at Jackie. She's huddled on

my couch, separating her hair into impossibly small strands for braiding. There seems to be no rhyme or reason and I cringe thinking of the ratted mess she would have were she still living.

"You know, I thought it was unfair that I died so young," I muse, feeling ashamed. "I was so angry. Cancer felt real to me, like a killer who targeted me, singled me out without any care for the family that I was leaving behind. Can you imagine? I had no idea what I was talking about. I was so lucky. I died at home. I got to say goodbye to my kids. I helped Richard plan my funeral. My little sister Marla came from Arizona half a dozen times to visit in the last few months of my life."

Reif gazes up at the stars without answering.

"Thank you for coming today," I say. "What made you decide to join us?"

"I knew the only way you could visit her memories was with a therapist. Wasn't sure if you would have thought of that."

"I didn't even know it was possible."

"That's because your therapist isn't a pushy old coot who wants to find out all your secrets. Teresa is fine letting you explore your past on your own terms. Winston, however, is not."

"Huh. Well, thanks. You came on a little strong, but ultimately I'm glad you were there."

"You're...welcome?" He raises an eyebrow. "Were you that good at delivering mixed compliments in your former life?"

"I'm sorry, it's been a long day."

"Don't tell me you're tired."

"Not physically, no. But somehow, yes, I am. I think I might go to the Memory Bank myself to clear my head."

Reif frowns. "Weren't you just there the other day?"

"It's been a stressful couple of days."

"And you don't think there's anything wrong with responding to stress by visiting a past that you can't get back to?"

"You're right," I say.

Reif nods, satisfied.

"I think I'll go to Visions instead."

He sighs and I know what's coming. "Come on, Lorna. There's a reason they restrict it. It's not good for you."

"It's fine. Just because you don't have any ties to mortality doesn't mean that's any healthier."

Reif looks away, his jaw tight.

"I'm sorry," I say. "I don't want to argue with you tonight. I just don't understand how you can judge me when you don't even seem to be making an effort."

"I'm not judging you, Lorna. I think it's wonderful that you had such a great life. To be honest, I'm a little jealous." He runs his hand through his hair and sighs bitterly. "My ex-wife didn't even come to my funeral. Married for fifteen years and she couldn't change her Botox appointment to pay her respects."

The unexpected disclosure makes me want to comfort him in some way, to reach out and hold his hand, but I resist. "I'm sure it's not because of you. Whatever her issues were, you can't blame yourself."

"But I do. I was an unreliable drunk. And that's why I know how dangerous it can be to cling to what you can't have. Visiting the Memory Bank or Vision Station...that's a slippery slope."

I pull the blanket tighter as if to shield myself from the truth of his words. "Teresa says it's good to be curious about my past and my family's future without me. She says exploring it is essential to understanding my pain and letting it go."

"But are you trying to let it go? Or are you just holding on tighter and tighter?"

I don't answer. I know I need to let go. But in this moment, it's the last thing I want.

In spite of Reif's warning, I leave for the Vision Station first thing the next morning. I pass through the Arrivals Plaza where a young man is bouncing on his toes impatiently while waiting at a gate. I think again about Jackie's arrival.

Why wasn't someone notified to meet her? In three years, I've never heard of someone being forgotten. Is there a chance that her death was unexpected and there wasn't time to prepare? But I've known plenty of people who died in accidents and still had someone there to greet them. Death is never truly unexpected in the afterlife.

Who's in charge of coordinating the Arrivals anyway? This opens a whole bunch of questions that won't go anywhere. I know, because I've already tried. In three years, I've had dozens—maybe even hundreds—of conversations with other people: Memory Facilitators,

Vision Coordinators, and a handful of counselors. No one knows who makes the laws concerning our world. No one knows what happens when we pass on. There are rumors, but they're contradictory and reflect mortal misconceptions and speculation.

All we know—all we believe—is that passing on is the only way not to be stuck here forever. And in order to pass on, we have to learn to let go of whatever is keeping us here.

Maybe for Jackie, it's the need for justice.

For me, it's something else.

"I want to see my family," I tell the Vision Coordinator.

"Who in particular?" she responds, her skin showing the tell-tale sheen of someone who will be passing on in a matter of days. Maybe even hours. I wonder what her story is. How long has she been here? What did she let go of?

"It depends on what they're doing."

"Let's see," she says amiably, tapping her tablet. "You're in luck! Mindi is at a volleyball tournament and Richard and Alex are there to watch."

"Perfect." I love to watch Mindi play volleyball. She works so hard and each year the team relies on her more and more.

I exit the car and step out into a gym echoing with the sounds of squeaking sneakers, the dull smack of a volleyball, and spontaneous cheers from the crowd.

The gym is enormous, with two volleyball matches going on simultaneously. I scan the area nearest me and see Mindi at the net jumping for a block.

I feel a flare of excitement. She's so tall now, with an effortless beauty that shines in moments like this when she's totally focused and unaware of anyone watching her. She's shed the softness of childhood and is adopting the angular features of her father. She tosses her long ponytail behind her shoulder and grins at a teammate, her white teeth perfect and gleaming. When did she get her braces off? Sometimes I spend so much time in Memories I lose track of how much time has passed for my family.

I ache to go to my daughter. To hear her laugh directed at me. To have her long arms thrown around me in an excited hug in the same way she hugs her teammates after a kill. I want to hear all about her life—her wins and losses, her joys at school, her heartbreaks, her hope.

Instead, I wander through the court, trying to be as near her as possible. But of course she doesn't know I'm there. Her whole attention is focused on her mortal surroundings.

A whistle blows and Mindi is rotated out.

"Nice job, Preston!"

I know that voice.

I lift my eyes to the bleachers and find Richard immediately. He claps as Mindi takes her seat, and she turns around and smiles.

Richard looks older than I always think of him. No matter how many times I see him in a Vision, I still remember him the way he looked when I was alive. Now he has more wrinkles and thinning hair, but he still looks as handsome as ever. He must be working out again because his broad chest is well-defined under his t-shirt.

That's good. It's good that he's taking care of himself again.

A sandy haired young man moves through the bleachers and sits next to Richard, soda and nachos in his hands. It takes me a second to recognize Alex from the back; he's grown so tall recently. His hair curls around his ears and hangs in his eyes and I'm seized with the urge to push it away so I can see his face. But it's clean, so I know the style must be a conscious choice and not a symptom of neglect.

I move up the bleachers and stand in front of them as they watch the game. They chat about the players and where in the tournament rankings a win will place the team. A book sits next to Richard on the bench, and the name on the spine makes me sad. Now that I'm gone, he's buying his favorite Gerald Houston books himself. I used to give him one as a gift each birthday or Christmas, and Houston was such a prolific author I never ran out of options. I wonder if this one is any good. He would tell me all about it if I were able to ask.

Currently, the book is forgotten as Richard helps himself to Alex's nachos.

They seem happy.

I'm glad.

And also miserable.

The crowd claps and whoops, and I realize that the match has ended while my back was turned.

Richard stands and stretches. "I'll be back in a minute, Alex. I need to make a call."

I turn and see Mindi gathering her gear with her teammates. Judging by their cheerful expressions, they must have won the match.

A group of teenagers approaches the girls. Some of them I recognize from when I was alive. Boys drape their arms over some of Mindi's teammates' shoulders. Boyfriends.

Looking for Mindi in the cluster of kids, I see her talking to a boy who has the build of a football player. I'm glad that he isn't touching her so familiarly, but from the way her face lights up, it's clear how she feels about him. He tugs on her ponytail, and she pushes him away, laughing.

I glance around the room looking for Richard. Does he know this boy? Can he see the signs? Who will help Mindi navigate her first romantic relationship?

Richard is nowhere to be seen. I move out into the hallway—passing through the doors without opening them—and find him near the entrance. His voice echoes against the cavernous ceiling.

"The championship game isn't until seven, so you'll have time, right?"

Pause.

"Of course. I'll let you know. But we already beat them twice during the season, so I think we'll make it."

He kicks idly against the base of a trophy case while he listens.

"Yeah, I think she'd like that."

Pause.

"Me too. Bye."

Richard slips his phone into his pocket with a smile and walks back to the gym.

I don't know what *me too* refers to, but I know that smile.

And I feel sick.

Nine

There are benefits to being dead. Not crying when your heart is breaking is one of them.

Reif and Jackie are waiting for me when I step out of the car at the Vision Station.

"Whoa! What's wrong?" Reif says when he sees my expression.

"Nothing," I say. That familiar tightness in my throat tells me I would have been on the verge of tears if I were still mortal.

"Bull," Reif mutters. "You wanna talk about it?"

I shake my head. "What are you two up to?"

"I wanted to meet Jackie's friends. You wanna come?"

No, I don't want to come. I want to go home and fix a mug of hot chocolate with cream. I want to cry and be held by Richard and hear him tell me how much he loves me and how he'll never love another.

"Yeah," I say. "But I think Jackie only has about fifteen minutes of vision time left."

Reif waves his fake ID badge at me. "Not anymore. Turns out that with the right connections you can transfer unused minutes from one person to another."

His smile irks me. He who never uses his vision minutes and then laughs at me when I do.

I follow them onto the car and avoid their eyes as we move out of the station to make our way to Seattle.

Within moments, the car stops and Reif and I follow Jackie into a paneled room furnished with couches and bean bags. Thick shag carpet in dark brown adds to the feeling that we've stepped back in time to the Seventies. A young man sits on the couch, his arms wrapped around a shockingly pale young woman wearing a beanie and a baggy sweatshirt.

Jackie's face brightens in recognition. "Hey guys," she says softly. She looks at me as if making introductions. "Raylene and Vince. We just call her Ray."

"Of course I told them," Ray is saying. "I mean, before it was like, maybe they don't need to know. But now that they found her body, what good does it do?"

Vince sighs and leans his head back against the arm of the couch. "I know. It's stupid. I just—I'm eighteen, you know. Stuff counts now."

"It was just a few pills. If it helps them catch who did this, don't you think it's worth it?"

"Sure. Of course. Poor Jackie."

Reif raises an eyebrow at Jackie. "Pills?"

Jackie bites her lip. "I...I might have given them some of my old meds."

"What sort of meds?"

"Just stuff left over from when I got my wisdom teeth

out and a couple of things I found in my mom's medicine drawer. Nothing big."

"Were you in the habit of giving pills to your friends?"

"Nah. They only asked a couple times. It wasn't a big deal. And besides, we didn't need them anymore."

Reif shoots me a look, but doesn't say anything else.

In the silence, Ray asks, "Do you think it's anyone we know?"

"Maybe." Vince rubs his stubbly chin against her beanie. "They say that more violent crime is committed by people we trust than total strangers."

Ray shivers. "I wish I'd never told her to meet us at the theater that night."

"It's not your fault. Who's to say she was kidnapped there anyway? It might have happened right outside her house. Maybe he was waiting for her. Maybe it's someone she asked for a ride."

"I wish they could find her phone."

"Not me. I'd hate to think of all those stupid videos she took of us."

"Vince!"

"Come on, she always had her phone out filming everything we did. It's like she was obsessed or something."

"It was cute. She wanted to be like us, that's all."

The condescension in their tone makes me cringe. I avoid looking at Jackie, trying to keep my expression neutral.

"She was a cute kid; it's true. But you've gotta admit it could be annoying sometimes. Always wanting to take selfies with us like she was a ten-year-old with her first phone."

"Vince!" Ray sits up and elbows him hard. "She was sweet and innocent and didn't deserve what happened to her!"

"Did I say she did?"

"Could you at least wait until they've had a chance to bury her before you start bagging on her like that? I liked her, and not just because she always had some extra cash on her or could score us some pills." Pink spots of color appear in Ray's cheeks.

Vince tries to grab Ray's shoulders, but she shrugs him off. "Don't be like that, Ray. You know I liked her too, but is it so bad to admit that it's nice to be just the two of us again?"

Ray shoots off the couch so fast that Jackie stumbles back in surprise.

"You make me sick."

"Come on, Ray! I just meant that I've missed you!"

Ray flips him off as she climbs the basement steps.

Jackie turns on her heel and heads back to the car.

I grimace at Reif, then hurry after her.

"Ray seems nice at least," I offer as I step inside the car.

"Yeah," Jackie mumble. "Yeah, she is."

Reif says nothing, but I can read in his eyes that he's as unimpressed with Jackie's friends as I am. We travel only a short distance before the car stops. When the doors open, we've arrived at a tidy little house with a small porch. An old Halloween jack-o-lantern sags wearily on the top step.

A chain link fence surrounds the small yard and next to the gate, flowers, stuffed animals, and balloons in the shape of a heart are piled on top of each other.

An unmarked police car is parked at the curb.

Jackie reaches for the gate and sighs dispiritedly when she can't grasp it. After a pause, she passes through the fence and up to the porch. I follow, but Reif takes his time, looking around the yard and viewing the house from several angles.

"Which window is yours?" he asks Jackie.

"It's in the back."

"How did you sneak out that night?"

Jackie doesn't answer right away.

"Your mom didn't know you left, right? So how did you sneak out?"

"The screen door squeaks so I used my bedroom window. It's not that far from the ground."

"Can you show me?"

We round the corner of the house and find a plastic lawn chair sitting under a dark window.

"Your mom didn't notice this here?"

"She doesn't spend a lot of time in the yard."

As Reif gets down on his hands and knees to examine the ground cover and spindly roses beneath the window, I feel a surge of irritation. He's making a fool out of himself, playing detective like this. I want to help Jackie as much as—no, probably more than he does, but you don't see me pretending like I'm on the set of *Law and Order*.

"What does your mom do?" I ask Jackie, trying to

focus on something else to stop from telling Reif what I think of his theatrics.

"She teaches at the local college. Head of the Business Department, actually," she says with a hint of pride.

"Nice. And, your dad...?"

"They divorced when I was six. It's just Mom and I. Or... it was. I guess now it's just her." She frowns and looks away.

"You wanna go inside?" I feel weird inviting myself in, but I don't want to watch Reif playing Cops & Robbers anymore.

Jackie and I enter the house through the screened porch in the back. We pass by flip-flops and Converse shoes by the back door—the red ones I'd seen her in the first day she arrived. I wonder how long it will be before Jackie's mom cleans them up. How long will she step over them and around them so that she can be reminded that once her daughter lived and breathed and had the luxury of thoughtlessly leaving her shoes lying around?

The back door leads into a snug dining room with white painted wainscoting and a tear-drop shaped chandelier. At the kitchen table, Mrs. Renfro pours coffee for two detectives.

"—don't have any reason to think that the killer was specifically targeting Jackie," one of the detectives is saying. He has neatly trimmed black hair and a deep dimple in his chin. "But until we find her phone, we can't say for sure. Jackie's friends say she didn't have a boyfriend, and they aren't aware of anyone she would have contacted that late at night."

"Besides them, you mean? Clearly I wouldn't know."

Jackie winces from the bitterness in her mom's tone, her guilty expression evident despite its translucence.

"We talked to everyone on the list you gave us and got pretty much the same story. Good kid, worked hard at school, friends on the yearbook staff, no history of boyfriends or partying. These two friends of hers are the only thing that don't really fit the mold."

"Do you think they're lying?"

"Not necessarily, but we're digging into their stories a bit deeper just to be sure. At this point, we can't rule anyone out."

"And what about DNA evidence? Chief Martinez said you would be able to get some…"

Off the body, she didn't say.

"Yes, we'll be sending whatever we collect to the lab. But you have to understand that DNA science isn't like a crystal ball. We've got a lot of samples to work with, which is good. Contamination and other things can interfere, so the more the better."

Mrs. Renfro looks sick. "I'm sorry, gentlemen, but I can't agree that having lots of DNA samples of my daughter's killer is a good thing. Not when I know what happened to her to make those samples possible."

The room grows still. Jackie picks anxiously at her lower lip.

"I wish they didn't tell her," she says. "Why did they have to tell her everything?"

"She's your mom," I say. "Of course she wants to know." But even as I say it, I wonder what I would do if it were my daughter. Would I want to know all the details?

Yes. Because if she suffered them, then the least I could do is have enough respect to listen.

But the thought of sitting with two detectives discussing the violent murder of either Mindi or Alex is too much. Especially after having just seen them in the flesh.

"I think I'll go check on Reif. Make sure he isn't getting up to too much trouble. You okay in here alone?" I ask.

Jackie nods, and I slip back outside. I find Reif under a window next to the porch. He glances up as I approach.

"Is Jackie with you?"

"She's still inside."

"I was hoping I could compare these footprints against her foot. Make sure she was the only one standing under this window recently."

I look at the ground, but can barely detect a slight impression of something that might be a shoe.

"There are a few shoes by the back door, but fat lot of good that does us, Sherlock. Since, you know, we're not corporeal or anything."

Reif smirks. "If we were corporeal, we couldn't be sitting out here under a dead girl's window without attracting attention."

I look again at the impression. "I can think of other things I'd rather be doing if I had a body right now."

"Oh yeah? Like what?"

"You're kidding me, right?"

"No, really." Reif straightens and looks at me with interest. "What would you be doing right now if you had a body? Right now in this exact moment."

I look up at the gray sky. "I'd probably be at my daughter's volleyball tournament. Or going to lunch with the team while they wait to see who they're playing in the championship tonight."

"Really? That's what you would most want to do right now if you had a body? Man, talk about small dreams."

"Hey, you asked, and that's probably exactly what I'd be doing."

"Yeah, but what would you *want* to do? If you didn't have to worry about volleyball tournaments and championships and an all-you-can-eat pizza buffet, what would you do right now if you could have a body?"

I smile. "I would run down that street all the way to the end as fast as I could until my lungs felt like they were going to burst and my heart beat out of my chest. Then I would eat a juicy hamburger with onion straws and bacon and steak fries and a vanilla milkshake."

Reif nods, impressed. "That sounds more like it."

"What about you?"

"I think I'd start with a smooth hazelnut cappuccino and then see where it goes from there."

I snort. "Speaking of small dreams. Come on, Reif. What is it you really want? What's keeping you here? And don't give me some glib response about lattes or cappuccinos. You've been here long enough that I'm sure you and Winston both know what it is that's holding you back."

"Sure we do. I'm here to annoy Winston enough that he'll pass on sooner to get away from me."

I laugh. "Do I need to talk to Winston to get some dirt

on you? Apparently there's no such thing as client privilege here."

"You could try," Reif says with a smile. "But to be honest, I'm not sure even Winston knows."

"But you do?"

He shrugs. "I have a hunch. But I could be totally off. Either way, knowing doesn't seem to be helping."

"But you do want to pass on?"

"Of course! Don't you? I mean, this world is great and all, and I do miss mortality. But if there's something better ahead, don't you want to find out what it is?"

"I don't know," I answer honestly. "I've never been very adventurous, I guess. What if it means forgetting my family? What if it means they'll forget me?"

"Impossible."

I purse my lips, surprised by his confidence. "Why do you say that?"

"Because your brain is sitting in a grave somewhere turning to worm food, and yet here you are with all your memories and feelings intact. There's gotta be a reason for that. I can't believe you'll lose those feelings when you pass on. If anything, you probably need them for something. Hey, maybe you get to be a Guardian Angel or something!"

I grimace at his mocking tone. The truth is, I like that idea. Sure, it's nice to be able to visit my family through visions, but I can't do anything to help them. I can't influence the physical world or appear to them or even pick up a shoe and bring it over to match a footprint in the soft loam.

In mortality, I heard hundreds of stories of people

who had visitors or divine help from the other side. No one had a good explanation for it, and I was always pretty dismissive about the whole thing. But those stories seem a lot less far-fetched now that I'm here.

"Can I tell you something?" I ask.

"Of course."

"Promise not to laugh."

"I'll try."

"I think Richard is seeing someone."

Reif's smile fades. "Ah. That explains your 'crisis face' when you got back from your vision. How do you feel about that?"

I sigh. "Like he's cheating on me."

"Lorna—"

"I know, it doesn't make sense. But you asked how I feel, and honestly, it feels like betrayal."

"It's been three years. Most people would think that's more than enough time."

"I know. And I agree intellectually. I know it's for the best. I know it's not fair to expect him to be alone, and I know it's good for the kids to have a mother's influence. But I feel in my heart like it's selfish betrayal. Like he's moved on and forgotten me."

"He'll never forget you, I promise. But don't you think moving on is a good thing? Don't *you* want to move on?"

I look at Reif incredulously. "Why would I ever want to move on? He was the love of my life! I love him just as much now as I did twenty years ago when he asked me to marry him. It breaks my heart to think he doesn't feel the same way."

Reif's expression clouds over. "I'm sure he does feel

the same way. A part of me will always love my ex. No matter the ugly years at the end, we had some great ones before that. I would say the best parts of my life were largely because of her. But somehow we move on anyway. We leave behind the pain and take the good with us to make our lives better."

I want to tell him that it isn't the same. That Richard and I love each other more than he loved his wife, or else why did he get divorced? But I know he can't understand. He can't know how hard it is to leave behind someone you loved that much.

"Thanks, Reif," I say instead. "I guess I still need to work on that."

Ten

Some people have jobs here, but they aren't like paid careers. There are those who work as therapists, and others who help us navigate the logistics of seeing Memories or Visions. But in a world where all our needs are met with a thought, that leaves no need for everyone to have some sort of occupation. I've never asked, but I assume that those who choose to volunteer do it because they don't like being idle. Or maybe it's part of their therapy.

It's a strange feeling to not contribute, since I spent so much of my life working in one capacity or another. Even in the years when I wasn't employed outside the home, I worked harder than ever. So I've decided that this probably isn't intended to be the final state of things. I wonder sometimes what sort of occupations lie ahead of us when we pass on.

Do they give us career aptitude tests like you take in high school? I can just imagine how that would go.

"Mrs. Preston, you have demonstrated a strong aptitude for rainbow creation, but your hatred of rainy climates makes *that a challenging match. You might consider applying to the Unicorn division."*

Too mythical? Yeah, well, I'm dead. Get over it.

"I'm inclined to agree with the cops," Reif says, standing back and looking at the list he's written on his sliding glass door.

We're gathered in his room, where he's procured a dry erase marker and is using his glass door as a whiteboard. He's listed everything we know, including what Jackie learned by listening to the detectives talk with her mother. They discussed the security footage from the parking lot that showed Jackie's abduction. Unfortunately, the cameras were old and poorly positioned, and her killer was hidden in shadow much of the time. Very little of him or his vehicle showed on the tape.

Jackie - 16 yrs old
    Good student
    Mom single
    No siblings
    Home alone
    Yearbook
    Older friends
    No known enemies

Murderer -
    Male
    Larger and stronger than Jackie

> Prepared (pillowcase, ligatures)
> Drives truck
> Movie theater late at night
> Violent sex offender - probably not first time?

Reif taps his lower lip with the marker. "He must have been out looking for a victim. You only knew ten minutes earlier that you were going to meet your friends. There was no way for him to know you'd be there."

"So it was a random stranger?" Jackie sits on Reif's couch with her legs crossed, hugging a pillow to her stomach.

"Not necessarily. Just because he wasn't targeting you doesn't mean he didn't know you. You were alone in that parking lot for several minutes before he grabbed you. Was he trying to work up the courage? Did he know you and that gave him cold feet?"

"I can't decide if it's better or worse if he knew me," Jackie says.

"My point is that we can't rule out anyone you know. But it's also likely that he was a total stranger, and we don't want to waste too much time trying to pin it on a classmate or a teacher."

"It's too bad we can't access the cops' sex offender database," I note.

"They said they were interviewing all the ones who live around there. But so far they don't have any promising leads," Jackie says.

The room falls silent as we each mull this over. Jackie picks absently at her lip. She's been even more subdued than usual after visiting her mom's house.

Reif speaks first, and his voice holds a note of apology. "The cops will be able to do a much better job working in the mortal world than we can. But you know where we have an advantage?"

Jackie nods, then buries her head in her arms.

"I'm so sorry, Jackie," I say.

She holds still for a moment, then raises her head and glares at me. I brace for an angry outburst, the kind I'd hear sometimes when my kids were frustrated and looking for someone to blame. But I'm not the target of Jackie's anger.

"I'll do it," she says fiercely. "He can't hurt me anymore. I want to find him. I have to."

Reif reaches out as if to lay a hand on her shoulder, then stops himself. "All right, then. The Memory Bank it is."

"I wish Reif and I could visit your memories without you having to be here."

I look questioningly at Reif, but he shakes his head.

Jackie steps into the Memory room with a look of cold determination on her face.

"Let's visit the moment when you regained consciousness," Reif says, handing his card to the Memory Facilitator, a thin woman whose green eyes are accentuated by cat eye glasses.

She glances at the three of us. "This memory has been flagged as particularly traumatic. Are you sure you want to continue?"

Jackie nods. She doesn't seem capable of speech.

"You know how to end the memory if it becomes too much? You can command the simulation to 'Stop' or you can simply exit the room." The worker looks at me meaningfully. "Stay close to her," she whispers as she passes me on her way out.

With dread, I drag two chairs over from the corner. Jackie and I both sit, but Reif remains standing.

"Memory commencing," announces a disembodied voice from an invisible speaker.

The room darkens to total blackness. Instinctively, I reach for Jackie's hand. She grips mine with both of hers, not even flinching at the dissonant thrum.

A low, steady hum fills the room, together with the sound of breathing. Irregular and labored, it continues for several minutes.

"Memories are limited to sight and sound," Reif says softly. "Can you remember what else you felt when you woke up? Could you tell where you were? Sitting or laying?"

Jackie's voice is tight and hesitant, as if she's struggling to breathe. "Laying down. On the floor of a van, or truck, I guess. The detectives said it was a truck."

"In the bed?"

I feel Jackie move, then she realizes we can't see her gestures.

"No. It was cold, but not that cold," she explains. "I must have been on the floor of the cab. When I moved around I felt the bars—seat supports?—against my back."

We listen for a few more minutes to the rhythmic

drone of the road noise and the panting struggle of Memory Jackie.

"My hands were tied up behind me. But not rope, something sharp and hard."

"Zip ties," Reif murmurs.

"My feet weren't tied, though, so I tried to feel around with them. I felt the wall of the truck and some trash, I guess, but nothing helpful."

As she says this, the sound of rustling paper comes from the darkness off to our right.

Then a man's voice speaks, startling Jackie and me.

"You awake then, cupcake?" he says.

The sound of Memory Jackie's breathing quickens.

"Don't worry now, we'll be there soon."

"Who are you? Where are you taking me?" Memory Jackie says, her voice muffled by the pillowcase and nearly drowned out by the truck's engine.

The road noise changes in pitch as the truck slows down and changes to the unmistakable grinding sound of tires on an unpaved road.

The helplessness of the situation washes over me as if I, too, am in the truck with Jackie. How long have they been driving? How far from the city are they?

"When was the last time it rained?" Reif asks.

"Uh, I don't know," Jackie says. "Maybe last week? Why?"

"The pavement was dry at the mall, but if it's rained recently enough, the truck would be leaving tire prints on the dirt road."

I wish he would keep these details to himself, even though that's why we're here. I'm strung so tight with dread, I can only imagine what it's like for poor Jackie. For Reif to make calm observations like that feels insensitive.

A squeal of brakes and a gasp from Memory Jackie tells me the truck has stopped. We listen in silence, senses attuned to every sound.

The click of a seat belt release.

The sound of a door opening.

The shifting of a body as the driver climbs out of the cab and slams the door shut again.

Memory Jackie's breathing accelerates.

The click of another handle and swinging of the door.

"All right, cupcake. Time to get better acquainted."

Memory Jackie grunts and moans and a scuffling sound makes it clear she's resisting as he bodily hauls her out of the truck.

"Help! Someone help!" Memory Jackie screams.

The man oomphs. Then a thump and Memory Jackie cries out.

"You gotta play nice if you want me to play nice too. Unless you want me to play rough. Is that how you like it?" His voice holds a slight drawl and I immediately think of the wide open spaces of Montana where I lived, picturing him with a mullet and cowboy boots.

"Please, just let me go," Memory Jackie begs, her panting loud through the pillowcase. "I just want to go home."

"Now, shh shh," the man says soothingly. "We're miles and miles outside the city. There's no one around, so you might as well save your breath."

Jackie's hand trembles in mine.

For a moment the only noise is the heavy breathing of Jackie's attacker as if his mouth is near her ear.

"Now there. See, that's better. Isn't that nice?"

Memory Jackie whimpers and I tighten my grip on Jackie's hand.

"I have something very special for you. But let's get you more comfortable first."

Memory Jackie yelps at the same time that Jackie next to me jumps up.

"I can't! I can't!" Jackie cries. "His breath is so awful! And his hands—No! I won't do this again!"

She flees out of the room.

Lights immediately turn on. Reif's eyes meet mine, and in them I see the horror that is surely reflected in my own.

I find Jackie hiding in the covered tube of a playground slide. I sit down at the mouth of the tube and wait for her to acknowledge me.

When she doesn't speak, I say, "You have got to be one of the bravest girls I've ever known. I was terrified myself in there. I don't know how you stood it so long."

She sits curled in a ball, her arms wrapped around her knees.

"Reif and I have been talking. I know you really want to figure out who did this to you. But have you ever thought it would be best to just leave it up to the police? You heard them, they've got lots of DNA evidence. It's only a matter of time before they catch this guy."

Jackie doesn't respond.

"I'll talk to Teresa again and see if there's someone you can talk to. Maybe it would be best to focus on letting go. This can't be good to make you relive it. Especially so soon after…"

Jackie still doesn't answer.

How can I reach her in her pain? My heart aches for her with an intensity that suggests if her murderer stood before me I could kill him with my bare hands. But how to help Jackie heal? How to find words that don't sound like empty platitudes?

I sit with her in silence until the sun sets in the distance, bathing the area in a golden autumn light.

"Jackie, let's go." I reach out and rub her back. Startled, she looks at me, her eyes bleary.

"Lorna! You're here."

"Yes, I've been here for hours. Did you not know?"

She shakes her head.

"Oh. Did you hear anything I said?" I ask.

"No. I wasn't really—"

"It's okay. I wondered if maybe this is too much for you, trying to find your killer like this. Maybe it would be good to leave it alone. I don't think it's helping you and there's nothing we can really do anyway. The police know what they're doing, certainly more than we do."

"Reif's a policeman."

"Huh?"

"Reif's a policeman. A homicide detective."

"How do you know?"

Jackie shrugs. "I can tell. Watch him. He's done this before."

I think about how Reif only became interested in helping Jackie after I told him Jackie was murdered, and how cool and professional he is about the whole thing. "Maybe, I don't know. He doesn't talk much about his mortal life."

"Which also fits. Cops have to be pretty good at keeping secrets."

"I guess. Look, Jackie, I think you should consider leaving this in the hands of the living police. It's too traumatic for you, and there's no reason to put yourself through it. It's bad enough you lived through it once, I don't want to make you live through it again."

Jackie shakes her head decisively. "No way. I want to catch him and make him pay for what he did. I don't care what it takes."

"Listen to yourself! We can't catch him. Only the police can do that. There's no way to 'make him pay' for anything. We're dead!"

"Then I'll haunt him until he goes crazy."

"It doesn't work like that! We can't interact with the mortal world. I'm sorry, Jackie, but there's nothing good that can come from—"

"Oh yeah? Maybe you just don't want it bad enough. He stole my life, he stole my future, he stole everything from me. You'd better believe that I will figure out a way to put him through hell one way or another."

She ducks out of the tunnel and steps over me, stalking down the steps and off into the approaching dark.

Eleven

When you've been here as long as I have, you begin to see patterns. Patterns in behavior for new Arrivals, patterns in the seasons, patterns in the stars. There are even patterns for whom we associate with. I don't think it's a coincidence that I've only met people from the western United States.

What I don't understand is why. Familiarity? Giving people an instant way to connect by grouping them with others from the same region?

Logistics? Geographical proximity making transportation to Visions easier?

But the question that really gnaws at me when I think of these patterns isn't "why." It's "who?" Who has determined things need to be this way? Who makes assignments and chooses how those assignments will be performed? Who dictates the weather and seasons?

No one will tell me. No one seems to know.

I can't decide if it's better that way, like I'm being given *the chance to decide for myself, or if I'm being treated like a child who can't handle the truth. Either way, asking doesn't get me anywhere. So I've stopped asking.*

Yet every time I discover a new pattern, I can't help but wonder.

∼

"Is everything okay? You seem troubled," Teresa says as she ushers me into her office.

"Any chance you've found a counselor for Jackie? I'm trying to help her the best I can, but everything I'm doing is making it worse. She's so miserable and isn't at all interested in letting go."

"Can you blame her?" Teresa asks. "Her transition was particularly traumatic. She'll need some time to work through what she's feeling. Don't rush her."

I sit in the chair across from Teresa but can't relax. "But I shouldn't really be helping her at all, should I? I'm not qualified. I have no training for this."

"Do you care about her?"

"Well, yeah…"

"Are you willing to listen to her?"

"Of course."

"That's all you need to do. Just be her friend for now. That's what she needs."

I stare. Teresa gazes back, her eyebrows arched and unflinching.

"You're kidding me, right?" I scoff. "What she needs is someone who can help her heal from what she's gone through."

"I'm working on it, I promise. But in the meantime, keep doing what you're doing." Teresa sits up straighter and tucks a springy curl behind her ear. "Now, are we going to talk about you? I see you saw a vision yesterday. Do you want to talk about it?"

I narrow my eyes. "You already know, don't you?"

"I wasn't there."

"How do you know it was tough?"

"Isn't it always?"

I sigh. "It was great. The kids look good and seem happy. Richard is taking care of himself, I can tell. He doesn't seem so burdened."

"But...?"

"I think he's got a girlfriend."

"Ah." Teresa taps her lower lip with a long fingernail. "You knew?"

"I knew it would happen someday. To be honest, I'm surprised it took this long. Men who were as happy as Richard in their first marriages are more likely to marry sooner after losing their spouse. If anything, it's a compliment to you because that means his first experience was so positive that he wants to repeat it."

"But I don't want him to repeat it! I don't want to be replaceable. You say that like I should be grateful."

"You don't have to be grateful. You don't have to be anything. I know that you want what's best for your family. And although you can't be there for them, I know you understand the next best thing would be to have another woman in their lives that will fill that gap."

"But I don't want to be a gap!" I say, my voice rising. "Why can't anyone see that? I'm just a hole that needs to be filled? Twenty years of marriage and that's all I am? A gap?"

"I'm sorry, of course that's not what I mean. It sounds to me like this is touching on some serious insecurities for you."

"You think?" My throat tightens against the angry words pushing to be released. "I never chose to die. I never wanted to leave. That decision was taken out of my hands and now everyone agrees that the best thing is for them to replace me. Everyone except me. Why don't I get to choose? Where's *my* replacement husband? *My* replacement kids? I'm stuck here alone while they get to move on with their lives, and I get nothing! I can't even cry properly!"

"Yes, exactly!" Teresa leans forward eagerly. "It's okay to be angry. You've been robbed, I agree. You lost everything you care about. It's ugly and painful and unfair. It's normal to feel angry. It's okay to be angry at Richard. At your kids. At the doctors who didn't keep you alive. At the mortician who plastered you in that stupid lipstick."

In spite of the tension, I smile a little.

"At God?" I ask.

"Sure. God or the Universe or Whoever decided that your story would end with cancer. But here's the thing, Lorna. That's only one part of your story. It's not the end. Your story has continued! That was just the end of one chapter or one act. You're here now because there's more ahead of you. What do you want the rest of your story to say?"

I look at her, my lips parted but unable to speak. Teresa's brown skin is beginning to take on a shimmer.

The silence in the room feels electric.

"Teresa," I finally manage. "Look at you."

She glances down and her eyes widen in surprise. When she looks back at me, they hold a depth of something unfathomable. Dark and full of rich promise.

"Excuse me, Lorna." She stands abruptly. "I think... There are some people I need to see before..." She steps around the table and embraces me. I can't remember the last time I've hugged someone, because it feels so awkward in this world. But it feels different this time, as if a memory of physical contact has leaked through somehow.

Teresa's eyes shine. "Think about what I've said. You're welcome to come next time and see if I'm still here. But I suspect I won't be."

I feel a twinge of envy. "Thank you, Teresa. Good luck."

"It's been a privilege."

The shimmer grows rapidly until her skin is almost glowing when the door closes behind her.

I stand alone in her office for several long moments after she leaves. It's quiet and still with that intangible *something* in the air that always happens when someone is close to passing on.

Only after I leave do I remember that with Teresa passing on, I'll be starting all over again trying to find someone to help Jackie.

And myself.

∽

"I've got an idea."

Reif is smiling when he meets us at the steps to the Memory Bank.

"Jackie has to be with us in order to share her memories with us, right? But there's no law that says she has to hear everything."

He holds out what looks suspiciously like an iPod and sound-canceling headphones.

"What in the world? Where did you—? That's not possible!" I protest.

"Why not? We can create chairs when we need them, clothes at will—"

"Yeah, but not—"

"I'll try it," Jackie says, putting a stop to our argument by grabbing the headphones and heading up the stairs.

"I don't understand," I hiss at Reif as we follow her. "I thought I'd seen everything that was possible here. Next thing I know you're going to be coming up with food we can eat."

"I wish."

With the padded headphones fitted around her ears, Jackie sits in the chair and looks at us with trepidation. Shaking, she presses play on the iPod and closes her eyes, her brow furrowed.

"Did you bring any headphones for me?" I whisper to Reif.

He grimaces. "You don't have to be here. I can fill you in later."

"No. I don't want to leave her."

The room goes dark.

"You're so beautiful, cupcake. Your skin is so smooth."

As soon as the voice begins, I clutch Reif's arm, seeking comfort even in the uncomfortable dissonance of contact.

"Don't think about what he's doing," he murmurs. "Try and figure out what his voice tells us about him. How old is he? Where's he from? Does he know Jackie? Why did he choose her?"

Memory Jackie screams, but it's cut off by the sound of a thump.

"I told you not to make this difficult." The man grunts. He strikes her again and again.

Memory Jackie cries.

I bury my face in Reif's arm.

Please let it be over.

Memory Jackie screams again.

I try to imagine what her attacker looks like, how old he is, but I can't think clearly with the feeling like insects crawling down my spine.

Memory Jackie's scream chokes off and she gasps for breath.

Her attacker's breathing is heavy and punctuated with low growls. Like an animal.

In the darkness I almost expect to feel his hands grabbing me. His weight holding me down. His fingers tight against my throat. His breath on my face.

I cover my ears with my hands, pressing them against my head. I can't bear it. If I could find the door, I would run out of the room. But the room is dark. I'm trapped until it's over.

"Pause Memory," Reif says.

Light infuses the walls again and the reflective glow returns.

There's only Reif, Jackie, and me in the room. But my image looking back at me looks haggard. Ghastly.

I shudder.

"Are you okay, Lorna?" Reif asks.

"No. No I'm not okay." My voice is shaking.

Jackie watches me, her eyes locked on mine. She knows what I heard. I immediately feel ashamed. After all I went through in life, I thought I was stronger than this. I'm supposed to be helping her, not falling apart when she needs me.

"Do you want to step outside?" Reif asks gently.

I look at Jackie's eyes, black in the low light. She knows what's coming. This is her story. Who am I to think it's too horrible to bear? She had no choice.

"It's all right," I say, looking at her. "I can finish it."

Reif puts his arms around me and I don't pull away, even though he isn't Richard. Even though there's no real comfort to draw from his touch.

Twelve

I don't speak to Reif or Jackie after the memory ends. We leave the room and walk back to my place in silence, close enough to touch, but the space between us making me feel very much alone.

In my apartment, I change into comfortable fleece pajamas almost without thinking as soon as I shut the door. I collapse into the couch and wish desperately for a mug of hot chocolate.

When I close my eyes, I hear them. Jackie and her killer.

So I don't close my eyes.

I wish there is somewhere I can go. I wish Richard were here so I could tell him everything.

No, not Richard. I can't imagine telling him these things. In the life we had together, nothing like this ever touched us. We were safe. We were happy. We worried about having enough money for vacation and Alex's grades and whether our kids had friends at school. We never knew this kind of terror.

Suddenly, I long for that life again. More than ever before.

I stand up.

"Where are you going?" Reif asks.

"For a walk."

"Come on, Lorna. Don't do this now."

"Don't tell me what to do. Stay with Jackie. I'll be back later."

The Vision Station isn't very crowded at night. Since we can't see our loved ones while they sleep, there is very little to see and do. But I go in anyway.

"I want to see Mindi and Alex," I demand at the booth.

"You only have about three minutes left for this week," the Vision Coordinator says.

"I don't care."

"Well, Alex is unavailable. But Mindi is at a friend's house."

"Mindi, then."

I fairly run to the car in my eagerness, pulling my hair up in a messy bun while I wait to get to my Vision. When I arrive and the door opens, I'm taken aback at what I see. I stand in a private theater room outfitted with designer furniture and more electronics than my car was worth. None of Mindi's friends that I knew when I was alive had that kind of money.

On a large leather sofa, Mindi sits with the same boy I saw her with at the volleyball game. Only this time they don't look like they're still getting used to each other. His arm is around her and she nestles in against him. He's broad and tall and again I'm reminded of a football player.

I watch them uneasily. Does Richard know Mindi is here with this boy and no one else is around?

They're watching a movie that I don't recognize with an actor with sparkling eyes and a five o'clock shadow. He's arguing with a short fat man who appears to have him confused with someone else.

Mindi's boyfriend isn't watching the screen. He's watching Mindi, twirling her hair around his finger. He leans toward her and caresses her chin, turning her face toward him.

Something ugly rises up in me as they kiss.

Where is Richard? Why are they here alone late at night?

"Mindi, it's time to go home now. Hey!" I move toward the sofa, clapping my hands, but of course they don't respond.

They continue kissing, their lips slurping and smacking unpleasantly in the manner of the inexperienced.

"This is my baby girl. Leave her alone!" I shout angrily.

Mindi and her boyfriend disappear into a wash out of white light.

"Your vision time has expired. Please return to the car."

"No! I can't leave her! She needs me!" I clench my fists and shout at the nothingness overhead.

All around me is white except for the car sitting open a few feet away.

"Bring her back! She doesn't know what she's doing!"

A part of me recognizes that I'm not being rational. That I'm reacting as much to the things I heard in Jackie's memory as I am to Mindi's first boyfriend making out with her alone.

"Please return to the car," the voice repeats overhead. "Your time has expired."

"Shut up! Just shut up! I know my time has expired! It expired three years ago and now I can't be here to keep my girl safe!"

I slump to the floor, leaning against the car. Somewhere in front of me, my Mindi is letting a strange boy touch her and hold her. A boy who doesn't love her as much as he thinks and will probably only use her for his own pleasure. And I can't do anything to stop it.

And Richard? He's probably out on a date, happy for the kids to be gone for the evening so he can go out with his new girlfriend.

They need me. They all need me. And I can't be there.

I don't know how long I sit, staring at the white light between my feet, before the sound of an approaching car makes me look up in confusion.

My car is still here, sitting behind me, the door open and the brightly lit interior visible. So who else is coming to this vision? Maybe it's a friend of Mindi's boyfriend. A grandparent or someone who just died and wants to check on him. Maybe the vision will turn back on and I'll get to see—

The door to the car slides open and Reif steps out.

I slump in disappointment.

"Hey, Lorna." He greets me with a sad smile.

"How did you get here? You're not supposed to intrude on someone else's vision if you're not invited."

"Maybe you don't know as much about this world as you think you do." He says it in a friendly way, not as a challenge, but it annoys me anyway. He looks around at the blank empty space. "Looks like your vision time expired."

"Yeah. It did," I say despondently. Then I remember something. "But you have extra time you could give me, right? Just like you gave Jackie?"

I scramble to my feet, but Reif eyes me warily.

"I don't think that's a good idea."

"Come on, Reif! I need this!"

"I don't think so. This isn't good for you. You've had a stressful day and need a chance to process what you've experienced. Wallowing in visions isn't the way to do that."

"It's not wallowing. Please? A few minutes, that's all. I just need to make sure Mindi is okay."

"Lorna, the whole point of these visions is to reassure you that your family is moving on so that you can too."

"Stop talking about moving on! I hate that everyone thinks moving on is such a good thing!"

"Isn't it? We can't change the past. We can only change the now."

"That sounds like someone who has been hiding from his own past. That's not healthy either."

"I'm not saying it is. I'm not talking about hiding from anything. I'm talking about accepting the past and then healing from it and letting it go. You can't change it. Holding onto it won't do you any good."

"That's easy for you to say when you didn't have anyone to hold onto!"

Reif blinks, and his blue eyes harden. "Wow. You really know how to go straight for the jugular, don't you?"

Shame pricks my conscience but I'm not ready to back down. "Stop trying to control me. I asked for your help, not a lecture."

"You think I'm being controlling? I'm not the one who's haunting my family and doesn't trust them to make any decisions on their own!"

"They need my help! Mindi has a boyfriend and Richard is totally oblivious—"

"Listen to you!" Reif says earnestly, stepping so close that I have to crane my neck to look up at him. "Didn't you ever keep things from your parents when you were a kid? Did they follow you to your boyfriend's house and spy on everything you did?"

"That's not the point—" I begin, but he ignores my objection.

"This is Mindi's life, not yours," he continues. "She needs to be allowed to make the same mistakes you made."

"But I don't want her to make the same mistakes!"

"That's not your choice! She needs to be given the

same freedom to totally screw up that you were given. Think about it. Look back on your life. Didn't the most important lessons you learned come from your worst mistakes or hardest times?"

I can't answer. Of course he's right.

"If you were alive right now, you would be sitting at home with Richard. And you would think about Mindi, sure. You might even be worried. But you couldn't do a whole lot about it because she's her own person and needs space to take ownership of her life."

The truth of his words twists painfully inside of me.

"It's just so hard," I whisper.

"Yeah, I know. Believe me, I know."

His eyes hold a depth of understanding I've never noticed before. I'm used to being the experienced one, the one who knows everything about this world. When did he surpass me in experience? How much more does he know?

"So how do I let go?"

"Well," he says, holding out his hand to help me stand. "We start by going back to the Station. And then, consider giving them some space for a while. No more visions. No more memories. Let's focus on helping Jackie. Then you can look forward and decide how you're going to continue your own story."

"My story?" I pause. "Teresa said something like that to me earlier today."

Reif smiles sheepishly. "Great minds think alike, I guess."

"Yeah, I guess. But shortly after she started talking like that, she started getting all shiny. I think she's probably passed on by now. She was changing pretty fast."

Reif's smile brightens. "Good for her! That's exciting."

"Yeah." I squint at him. "But don't you start getting any ideas of doing that to me."

"Doing what?"

"Passing on without any warning and leaving me behind."

Reif wraps an arm around my shoulders and leads me toward the door of the car. "I wouldn't dream of it."

Thirteen

No one really knows what it feels like to pass on. How could we? The only ones who've done it are gone. But if you stay here long enough, you hear the rumors. Some say that's when we meet God. Others say that's when we face judgment for all our wrongdoings. I expect it's a combination of both. How can you possibly be judged fairly if you're still holding onto the pain of life?

I've met those who think that after we pass on we get our bodies back, but they're not sick or old or hurting anymore. They're perfect and way cooler and stronger than they were when we were alive. It all sounds pretty metaphysical to me.

But then again, here I am writing to you on stationery that I just magicked into existence with my imagination. Who am I to talk?

"Did you find a new therapist?" Reif asks, looking over my shoulder.

"No," I reply, flipping the letter over.

"But you're still writing to your kids?"

"It's a good way to work stuff out. Have you ever considered how little we know about what comes next? It's all just rumor and guesswork. Doesn't that seem strange to you?"

Reif shrugs. "It's not too surprising considering the steps it takes to heal from trauma."

"What do you mean?"

"Well, if you think about it," he begins, sinking into the couch, "death is a traumatic event for all of us. Even if you live to an old age and pass away peacefully in your sleep, the process of this part of you—" he gestures to himself, "exiting your body and moving on to this place, that's a huge deal. And scary because we've never done it before and no one who has can tell us anything about it. So if someone's trying to heal from trauma, to say to them, 'Look, someday this thing that's eating you up inside is going to be no big deal. You'll be fine,' would be really unhelpful. Dismissive, even."

"Okay, sure," I say, clicking my pen rhythmically in the way that Richard always hated. "But how would telling us what happens when we pass on get in the way of healing?"

"Well, this is all just conjecture. But it makes sense that in order to help someone work through their trauma and heal from it, you don't distract them with a goal that feels impossible and unreachable. You just allow it to be what it is in the moment, gently helping them process it through lots of steps until they get to the other side themselves."

"But why not at least give us that glimpse so that we know if it's worth going through the steps?"

"That's just it. We can't skip any steps. We can't short-change the process. If getting that glimpse would make us either impatient—or even worse, *hopeless* because we can't see how we'll ever get there—then it's best not to risk that glimpse in the first place."

I frown. "That seems a pretty astute judgment for someone who's only been here for six months. What exactly did you do in your former life?"

Reif's smile widens. "I wasn't a therapist, if that's what you mean."

"Come on, tell me. You know so much about my life, but I know so little of yours."

"That's because I prefer this life to the last one," he says breezily as he stands. "Come on, Jackie's going to meet us at the Vision Station."

"There you go again, blowing me off. Come on, Reif. Why don't you trust me?"

He pauses at the door and looks back over his shoulder. "I do trust you. But the truth is that I'm ashamed. You already know how I died. That just about sums up my whole sorry existence."

I shake my head as I follow him to the door. "I don't believe it. What I know of you is a kind, funny, intelligent man who's always looking out for others. But not in a super annoying way. In a meaningful, I'm-glad-you-have-my-back kind of way."

Reif snorts. "Anytime now you're going to stop yourself before delivering those backhanded compliments."

I blink. "I did it again? Sorry!"

Laugh lines crease the corners of his eyes as he waves away my apology. "Really, Lorna, my past is best left in the past. Just be glad you didn't know me then."

"Well, I'm definitely glad I know you now. But I wonder if you talked about your past a little bit, maybe you could let go of it and get closer to passing on yourself."

"I think I pretty much let go of it as soon as I walked through that gate. Nothing more to talk about."

"It doesn't work that way," I insist. I lean one shoulder against the wall and fold my arms. "If your life was as miserable as you say, that's not something you shed so easily. You might ignore it. You might run from it. But you're definitely not letting go of it."

"Some people don't have as much to hold onto as others. Isn't that what you said yourself?"

Clearly he has no intention of telling me any more.

"All right, fine," I surrender. "I guess I'll just have to guess then. Jackie thinks you were a homicide detective."

"Oh yeah?" Reif reaches past me to open the door. He's so near that if we still had bodies I would be able to feel his warmth. "And what do you think?"

"I think you're way too cheeky to have worked homicide."

"Is that right?" His eyes glint with humor, like some private joke shared between friends.

Except I'm still on the outside.

"Maybe you worked the front desk," I say. "Never got your hands dirty yourself, but spent enough time around the real cops that you picked up a few things. Not enough to be really useful, of course. Just enough to make yourself look like an idiot when you try to solve mysteries as a ghost."

I pass through the open door and the sound of his bright laughter echoing down the hall makes me feel more alive than I have in days.

Jackie meets us at the Vision Station with her hands on her hips and annoyance practically crackling off her. "My mom doesn't have any appointments to meet with the cops today. How are we supposed to find out what's going on if they aren't telling her anything?"

"That's typical in an ongoing investigation," Reif says. "There can be a lot of ups and downs and false leads, and I'm sure they don't want to drag her through it all. Plus, they need to control what gets out to the news."

"Mom must be going crazy. How do we know they're even doing anything?"

"These things take time. It's not like on TV when they solve everything in fifty minutes."

"Yeah, I know. I'm not stupid," Jackie snaps.

"Is there anyone else we could visit that could help?" I ask.

"I don't know. My school...my friends...but I don't know that anyone there would know anything."

"I've got an idea," Reif says. He goes over to the counter and starts talking to the coordinator behind the window.

I shake my head. Reif is more excited about Jackie's life than he is about his own.

"How are you doing?" I ask Jackie while we wait. "How are you feeling? You're so brave about all this, but if at any point you decide it's not worth it, we can stop."

Jackie tugs at her long braid the color of an autumn sunset and tosses it over her shoulder. Today she's wearing a t-shirt that says *Life is better with a plot twist*. She has on black jeggings and a gray sweater. I find it encouraging that she's finally changed out of the clothes she'd worn since the day she transitioned.

"I don't want to stop," she says. "Not until we know who did this. And then, I want to help the police catch him."

"That might be a little more than what we can pull off," I warn. "I've told you before, there's no way to interact with the physical world."

"Reif said we can."

"What?"

"Well, maybe he didn't exactly say that. But he thinks that people who have passed on can interact with the physical world."

"There are rumors that crop up from time to time, but it's just conjecture. In any case, passing on means being able to put aside your pain and move on. Not searching for vengeance."

Jackie kicks against the curb. "I don't know why everyone makes such a big deal about moving on. As if I could ever just forget about it. "

I can't disagree because didn't I complain to Teresa about the same thing in our last session? Instead I wonder aloud, "Who's everyone? Have you been talking to other people?" That seems like a good sign. I thought Reif and I were the only friends she had.

She fiddles with her braid. "I met a couple of girls at the Arrival plaza the other day."

"Are they nice?"

"Isn't everyone? We're in Heaven, in case you hadn't noticed. Everyone has to be nice."

I ignore her snark because Reif is jogging toward us, his face split into a smile.

"Got it," he says, ushering us toward a waiting car. Jackie almost leaps aboard in her impatience.

"Where are we going?"

"It turns out that Lorna has a friend in the police department doing IT."

"What? I do?"

"Marcy Carpenter?" He brushes past me to step into the car.

"Marcy? Did she move?" The door seals behind me as soon as I step on.

"I have no idea." Reif says. "I just had the coordinator do a search for people connected to us who also work for the Billings Police Department, and you turned up a match."

"Billings? What are you talking about? How's that going to help? Jackie is from Seattle."

Jackie and Reif exchange a look of confusion.

"What? Why are you looking at me like that?"

"I grew up in Seattle," Jackie explains. "But I've lived in Billings for the past year. We moved there when Mom took the new job at City College."

"You're kidding me. I thought you lived in Seattle!"

"What difference does it make?"

"None, I guess," I lie. "Except that I'm from Billings. My family still lives there. How could I not recognize my hometown?"

"In fairness," Reif offers, "we haven't exactly been taking in the sights. A movie theater at night looks the same from one city to the next."

"Whatever, it doesn't matter. I just thought..." *That this was happening far away from the people I love*, I don't finish. I feel the sting of shame and look away.

The car stops and the door slides open revealing a small office filled with tall servers and scarcely room for a couple of desks. There sits my friend Marcy and an Asian man whose hair has the attractive rumpled look of someone who cares enough to look as if he doesn't.

Marcy is typing at her workstation, and her coworker is talking on the phone. We don't waste any time with them.

Reif moves past the desks to the door and I follow with a cheerful, "Hey, Marcy!" to my old friend.

Out in the hallway, we pause.

"So, where to?" Jackie asks.

"Well, we can only get so far away from the person we're connected to here. But this doesn't look like a very big station. I'll bet we can find the detectives—what were their names again?"

"Brown and Randolf."

The detectives aren't in, so Jackie and I go through Randolf's cubicle while Reif takes Brown's. We can't physically handle anything, but we don't need to. The desk is littered with useful information on their hunt for Jackie's killer.

On a notepad near the phone the following information is scratched down.

Ford F-150 w/shell
Black? Blue?
7C/0/G??8/0?A

A legal pad sits out on the desk with the name *Joy Sanders* written at the top. Scanning the notes, I gather that Joy is Jackie's yearbook advisor who recruited her the previous year because she learned that Jackie loved photography. A list of student names have little notes like "jealous?" "close" or "partner" scribbled in the margin. One, a boy named Trevor, has the words "sex off." written next to him.

"Do you know a Trevor from yearbook?"

Jackie looks up from the calendar she's examining.

"Trevor? Yeah, I know him."

"Is he...nice?"

"He seems okay. Kind of keeps to himself."

"This note looks like he's got a sex crimes background."

"What?" Jackie looks over my shoulder at the interview sheet. "Whoa, who would have thought?"

"Any chance he could be your killer?"

Jackie purses her lips. "I don't think so. I'd think I would recognize Trevor's voice. But that guy seemed older. And Trevor's a skinny kid. This guy wasn't."

Detective Randalf enters the room just then, totally oblivious that we're poring over his notes. We move away from his desk guiltily, even though he passes straight through us on the way to his computer.

He sits in his leather chair with a heavy sigh and reaches for his mouse.

Reif wanders through the cubicle wall to stand behind him. Even though I know Detective Randalf can't hear or feel us, it still feels invasive to me, but Reif doesn't seem to care about personal space.

"Look at this," Reif says, pointing to photographs Randalf has pulled up on the screen.

"They found my purse?" Jackie says, hurrying to look at the handbag that looks like it was once bright yellow but now is a soiled brown. Judging by the grate in the photo, I'm guessing it was stuffed down a storm drain.

"I wonder how they found it," Reif muses.

"Look! My phone!" Jackie says excitedly, pointing to a picture of a slim iPhone in a jeweled case.

"That's promising," I say, looking at Reif for verification.

He nods. "It should give them a better idea of where she was killed. Unless the killer ditched it soon after he grabbed her."

Detective Randalf pulls up a black and white photo of a pickup truck. The long cab gives it the impression of an SUV at first glance. It's blurry and pixelated and difficult to see.

"What about the DMV? Can't they search the records to track down the truck?"

"You don't have to whisper, Lorna."

"I know," I say sheepishly. "I feel weird being so close to a total stranger and invading his bubble like this."

"If he doesn't know, there's no invasion, right?"

"But *I* know. It's still weird."

I turn back to the picture on the screen. Now another photo has joined it, clearly a still shot from the night of the abduction. I peer at the grainy image.

"Why can't they clean up the photo like they do in the movies?"

"Because this isn't the movies," Reif says. "You can't zoom in on an image that doesn't have enough information to begin with. You get what you get."

I look at the license plate, impressed that they gleaned as much as they did. It looks like a shadowy blur to me.

"They can search DMV records, right?" I ask.

"Yeah, and an unsolved homicide will take priority. But it'll take time."

"That's what you say to everything," Jackie complains.

Reif gives her a half smile. "Real life investigative work isn't as sexy as it looks in the movies."

Detective Randalf picks up the phone and dials.

"Yeah, Bob, I've been looking at that truck again. There's a symbol on the bottom corner of that back window."

Pause.

"Yeah, I know. I'm wondering if it might be something else."

We all move closer to the computer screen to get a better look at what he's talking about. Something about it seems familiar.

"Can we have our computer folks look at it again? I

know it's not much to go on, but it looks to me like a decal was stripped off but they couldn't quite get it all. Yeah, like it peeled off the face and left part of the underneath layer behind."

All at once I recognize it, a pattern in shadows. "That's the symbol for the Rimrock Country Club."

"How do you know?"

"I worked there summers when I was in college. I'd recognize it anywhere. I did my last event there when I first started chemo. They were working on a rebrand at the time. That's the old logo."

Jackie looks expectantly at Reif.

Reif looks at me like Christmas has come early.

"Any chance you still know someone on staff?"

Fourteen

The Rimrock Country Club sits on an expansive green below the iconic Rimrock Bluffs in northern Billings. The sandstone cliffs are impressive at this distance, the afternoon light catching hints of ochre and crimson. It's been years since I've set foot here, yet now it feels like I've been transported back twenty years earlier to those summer days as a college student earning money for the next semester's tuition. Emotions wash over me as if it were yesterday. Excitement about life but afraid of it at the same time. A desire to be more than I was but keenly aware of my youth and inexperience. Thrilled about the possibilities of a life ahead of me.

How much shorter that life turned out to be.

The car brings us to the third green where a grounds worker is driving an aerification tractor in neat rows across the wide expanse of sod. Carl—my supervisor from more than twenty years ago—stands close by, gesturing widely as he converses with a young man dressed in jeans and a work shirt with the new RCC logo. Carl is substantially grayer now, his tidy beard sporting a generous sprinkling of white.

We waste no time with the grounds crew, moving instead toward the back of the newly renovated clubhouse. Well, it was newly renovated when I was alive, but that would be five years ago now. I coordinated the grand reopening, complete with formal dinner and a live band, as well as a special wall honoring significant donors with their names etched in glass.

We mount the stairs to the "fishbowl," a large circular room with floor to ceiling windows that offer a view of the green.

"Gravity works on us then, I guess?" Jackie says as she climbs the steps.

"I don't understand it either," I admit. "Apparently there are some laws of physics that apply when we're in this world. Or at least, echoes of them. You can even sit in a chair without passing through it, but I don't know if the chair is actually supporting you or if it's just your imagination copying the motion of sitting."

We pass through the clubhouse—literally pass right through the ten foot windows—with its dining room laid out for the dinner hour. Beyond that is a lounge with a large stone fireplace and shining tile floors. We ignore the handful of occupants there and make our way out the front door to the parking lot.

Only a few cars sit there, which is typical for a Tuesday afternoon. None of them are a dark Ford F-150 with a topper.

"Well, I guess it was a long shot."

"So now what?" Jackie asks.

"We could wait. But I'm not sure it would help. Things really pick up on the weekend. If we want to find his truck here, that'll probably be the best time to come back."

Jackie's face falls.

"I'm interested in checking out this Trevor guy in your yearbook class," Reif says. "Should we go to your school? We can always check back here later."

"Sure, I guess," Jackie says, but it's clear she's disappointed.

As we take the car back to the Station we all retreat into our thoughts, Jackie rubbing absently at her lower lip and Reif staring up at the ceiling. I don't need to guess what Jackie is thinking about, and Reif probably won't tell me if asked. As for me, I'm still troubled that I didn't realize that Jackie lived in Billings. Why didn't I recognize the theater plaza? To be fair, my family always went to the other one closer to where we lived. But it seems like I should have known.

I think back to our visit to Jackie's house. It could have been in a thousand different cities. And when we visited the police station, we only saw the interior. It could have been any police station in any town in the country. I don't follow local politics and have no idea what our current police chief looks like.

But it's unsettling to think I don't know my own hometown better. It's even more unsettling to know that there's a killer at large in the city where my family still lives.

"I guess one of the things that bothers me," I say suddenly, drawing looks from Reif and Jackie, "is that I assumed that the Seattle police would be better equipped to handle a murder investigation. Stuff like this doesn't happen that often in Billings. What if they mess it up? What sort of experience could have prepared them for Jackie's case?"

"Thanks a lot," Jackie says. "That doesn't make me feel better."

"Sorry. I just felt more confident when I thought there were some big city detectives working on your case."

Reif disagrees. "Just because they might not have a lot of experience doesn't mean they're going to screw it up. There are lots of resources they can turn to if they need it. I'm usually impressed with the character and tenacity of small town cops."

"And just how many small town cops have you had experience with?" I ask him meaningfully.

He winks but doesn't answer my question.

Jackie catches my eye and mouths, "Cop," with a knowing look.

At the Station, we get set up to visit Jackie's high school. The car drops us off in the middle of a nondescript classroom with no windows and desks that look like they came straight out of the Nineties. A woman with frizzy hair sits on the end of a table, her expression serious. Six teenagers are squeezed into the desks, some more comfortably than others, a few holding phones and one with a notebook.

"That's Trevor," Jackie says, pointing to the kid with the notebook.

I peer at him as the woman—whom I assume is Joy Sanders—speaks.

"I'm sure a lot of your parents are feeling the same way."

Most of the kids nod.

"My mom says I have to be home by dark and won't let me go anywhere unless she or Dad goes with me," a girl with black pigtails says.

"It's understandable. They're scared. We all are. But it's okay to be frustrated. Give them some time. It's hard for all of us to process Jackie's death, but it won't always be this way."

"I think we should do something to help," Trevor says. He has a narrow face and long legs that fold awkwardly under the small desk.

Joy Sanders blinks in surprise, making me wonder if Trevor doesn't speak up much. "That's very thoughtful of you, Trevor. What do you have in mind?"

He leans forward, his long arms gripping the edge of the desk. "I don't know. I just think we oughta do something. Jackie didn't deserve what happened."

The girls nod.

"We should add a memorial page to the yearbook," one suggests.

"Or hold a fundraiser to help pay for funeral costs."

Reif and I walk over to Trevor. He seems like a shy, nerdy type of kid who would always find himself on the fringes of any group he tries to join. It's a flash judgment and probably not a fair one, I realize. But once it comes, I can't shake the thought.

"I don't think he did it," I say, taking in his acne and dirty fingernails. "His voice is all wrong. Too self-conscious."

"Maybe," Reif says. "But it's hard to say how he might act while committing a violent act. In a twisted mind like that, it makes them feel powerful. Gives them confidence to act and even sound differently than he would in a class of his peers."

Jackie sits between two of the girls, listening to the conversation. Her eyes follow the flow of the conversation, her lips parted slightly as if she would love to jump in and add her own ideas.

I pitch my voice lower. "Look at Jackie, though. She doesn't seem threatened at all. I think if it was this boy, she would sense it."

"You're probably right," Reif says. "I wish we knew what sort of sex offense he's guilty of. I would feel better if we could rule him out once and for all."

"Well, the police already have their eye on him. I'm sure if there's any chance he did it, they'll figure it out."

Reif smirks. "Sounds like you do have some confidence in the Billings Police Department after all."

"I'm just saying," I say defensively, "that we're covering ground they've already covered. Or will cover soon. We really aren't adding anything to this investigation."

I turn away from Mrs. Sanders' saccharine smile and head for the door.

"Where are you going?" Reif asks.

"I'm going to check the parking lot. Might as well check to see if there are any vehicles that might fit the murderer's."

Reif doesn't object.

I walk out into the hallway and pause, wondering where I should turn. It's a long, institutional hallway lit with fluorescent lights that looks like it's desperately in need of a remodel. I turn right and head toward a wider space that I hope will lead to the entrance. Sure enough, the way ahead of me brightens as skylights and high recessed windows illuminate a large open common area leading to the exit.

I stop.

Ahead of me is a statue of a rearing mustang. The same statue that I've seen dozens of times in visions. And I know, even without looking, that if I turn around I'll see a mural of a giant Montana landscape with wild mustangs running at breakneck speed painted on the wall above me. Above the statue hangs the words South Billings High School.

I curse under my breath, feeling a surge of panic.

This is Mindi's high school. My own daughter is here, in these halls, possibly having class with a killer.

Fifteen

I spin around, as if expecting to see Jackie's murderer lurking in the halls right at this moment. Making a decision, I hurry through the outside doors to the parking lot beyond. It's packed, typical for a school day. Running, I race down the rows of parked cars, looking for Ford F-150's. There are dozens. Older models. Newer models. So many. This is Billings, after all.

I focus only on the dark-colored ones, but none of them have a topper. I finish one lot and begin on the far side of the lot behind the bus lanes. And then—

There it is. Not black. Not blue. But a dark, dirty green. Extended cab. Large shell covering the bed. License #7C 1601A

"Reif!" I shout in alarm.

He and Jackie are there in moments, standing next to me and staring at the truck.

Jackie swears much more eloquently than I. "He goes to my school? He knew me after all?"

"It looks like it," Reif says, his face grim. "Do you know what kind of car Trevor drives?"

"I don't know," Jackie says.

"You still think it could be Trevor?"

"Not necessarily," Reif admits. "But finding the perp is as much about eliminating leads as zeroing in on a single suspect. It wouldn't hurt to rule him out for sure."

"Maybe there's information in the truck that can tell us who it belongs to," I suggest.

I pass through the door, feeling a new desperation to find Jackie's murderer. He probably knew Jackie. He went to her school. She never suspected. She still doesn't know who it was. How can anyone be safe?

How can Mindi ever be safe?

Inside the cab of the truck are fast food wrappers and a newspaper loose on the floor.

"Look! A receipt! Oh, never mind, he paid with cash," I say with disappointment, glaring at the offending scrap on the floor.

"There's probably insurance and registration information sitting in that glove box," Reif says wistfully. "But I'm fresh out of mortal hands."

"Sometimes I really hate being dead," I growl.

"We've got to tell the police," Jackie says. "They still haven't found the killer's truck. If we could somehow lead them here, right now..."

"I wish," I say. "There's no way we could get that message across."

"How can you say that?" Jackie shouts. "Have you ever even tried?"

"Of course I've tried!" I insist, exasperated. "That's one of the first things everyone tries when they learn about the visions! Send messages to your loved ones. Haunt your old boss. I've heard it all, and I'm telling you, it doesn't work."

"She's right, Jackie," Reif says reluctantly, running a hand through his hair. "We don't belong to this world. Viewing it is all the access we're given. We can't interfere here any more than they can interfere in our world."

"Then what's the point? Why show us this if we can't do anything about it?" Jackie is almost screaming.

"I think the point is so that you can see for yourself that the people you love are going to be okay," I say, thinking of my family. "That someday they'll move on and you can too."

I know immediately it's the wrong thing to say.

Jackie rounds on me. "Okay? My mom is not okay! How can she ever be okay with what happened?"

"I'm sorry—"

"Would you be okay if it were your daughter who was raped and murdered and left in a dumpster at a rest stop?"

"No, of course not—"

"Would you be able to move on from that?"

"No, I didn't mean—"

"Then shut up and stop telling me to get over it!"

I clamp my mouth shut. Reif lays a hand on Jackie's arm, but she shakes it off. Her face is wracked with pain and anger.

I know pain. I know anger. But it's nothing compared to what Jackie is suffering.

"Then don't get over it," I say.

"What?" she demands, her braid snapping as she whips around to glare at me.

"Don't get over it. Don't try to move on. Embrace it."

"What are you talking about?" she asks, annoyed. But slightly less angry.

"What would you do if these restrictions didn't apply? Right now, what would you do?"

"I—" Jackie considers this. "I would tell the police where to find this truck. No. No, I wouldn't even do that. I would sit right here until he came out to the truck and find out who it belonged to. Then I would follow him home and give his name and address to the police."

"And then what? Would you be satisfied?" I push.

"I guess," Jackie says, calmer now. "Though evidence doesn't always convict someone, right? Sometimes they get off. Maybe I wouldn't even involve the police. Maybe I would just take care of him myself."

"Take care of him how?"

Reif's eyes flicker to mine uncertainly, but he doesn't interrupt.

"I don't know. Something long and painful. Tie him up to the back of his own truck and drag him for a while, maybe? If that didn't kill him, then I'd probably cut off some choice body parts and stuff them down his throat."

I grimace.

"I read that in a history book somewhere," she says defensively.

"Well, if anyone deserves something like that, it's

him. But would you actually feel better if you did all that?"

"Of course I would!" Jackie snarls.

"Would it make your mom feel any better?"

Jackie falters. "Probably not. She would want to see justice done. She doesn't really get into vigilante stuff."

"I hate to say it, but there's not a lot you can do for your mom. She's going to have to learn how to grieve and heal on her own."

"So, even if it doesn't help my mom, it would be worth it to me. And then he wouldn't be able to kill anyone else."

"I agree. I think it would be worth it too. Both for your sake and to protect other girls like you. But I think that's also one of the reasons why we aren't allowed to interact with this world. Just imagine if we could all enact our own personal vendettas with the kind of power we've been given here."

"I don't see a problem with that."

"Not when you're the one with the vendetta, no. But what about if it were someone else? What if your mom had a student who blamed her for a poor grade that ruined their chance of getting some job or internship or grad program and then decided to make her pay for it?"

"Well of course that would be different."

"Why?"

"Because a bad grade is nothing like murder."

"Okay, so you would allow murder victims to pursue their own personal justice, but no one else?"

"Maybe, I don't know."

"What about rape and sexual assault that didn't end in murder?"

"I would say yes."

"Okay, so all violent crimes then?"

"Sure, why not," Jackie says, crossing her arms with irritation.

"What about the accidental deaths? What about when some teenager is joy riding with his friends and misjudges a corner and hits and kills a father of three?"

"Look, what's your point?"

"My point is that the mortal world has a justice system for a reason. Maybe it's the same reason we can't exact justice here from our world. We don't have all the information, and we're bound to make mistakes. No one should be given that kind of power over another person."

"Why not? He used that kind of power over me."

"And it was a heinous crime that he will answer for," I say fervently. "I don't know if people like him will face a court in our world, but if they do, I'm confident that the evidence will be based on perfect truth and not limited to what's admissible in a mortal court."

Jackie looks deflated. "So I have to wait for God or whoever to make him pay?"

"Not necessarily. I'm sure the police will find him," I say more confidently than I feel. "They're looking in all the right places. They'll get there—I'm sure of it. But if something goes wrong and it turns out he's the mayor's son or something and they have trouble prosecuting him, I'm confident that he will still face justice. Sooner or later."

"How can you be sure?"

I pause, unsure why I feel so strongly.

"Because murderers don't come to our world," Reif interjects.

I turn to Reif in surprise.

Jackie blinks, her brown eyes hopeful. "They don't?"

"Nope. I've looked into it. Violent criminals go somewhere else. I don't know where. No one seems to know. But there aren't any in our world."

"So Hell's real? I guess that's something."

"Lorna's right, Jackie," Reif says. "It really is for the best that our worlds stay as separate as possible."

She falls silent and climbs up onto the hood of the truck, sitting with her shoulders hunched in a clear sign that our conversation is over. I watch her dark expression, wondering what sort of Hell she's imagining for her killer.

As we wait for the owner of the truck to appear, my mind wanders to Mindi. I've decided not to seek her out in any visions, but if we just happen to be there at her high school, there isn't any harm in it. Is there?

"Do you want to meet my daughter while we wait?" I ask Reif. "This is her school. She's probably here somewhere."

"I'd be honored, thanks."

Jackie shakes her head. "I'd rather just stick around here."

"Yell for us if you see anything."

As we head back to the school, I say to Reif, "I'm not sure lying to Jackie is the best strategy. She's pretty smart and we don't want to compromise her trust."

"What do you mean?"

"Telling her that violent criminals don't go to the same waiting place with the rest of us."

"I wasn't lying. They don't."

I glance at him, but he seems genuine enough. "Did someone tell you that?"

"Sort of. I figured out early on that there was an unusually high concentration of nice people here. So I talked to Winston about my suspicions, and he more or less confirmed that he's never known of anyone guilty of any serious crime coming here."

"You think they really go to Hell?"

"Not as such, no. But it might as well be. I think they go to a place like ours where they get the kind of help they need. Most violent criminals were victims themselves in some way, but they didn't get the help they needed when they were alive. My guess, and Winston couldn't confirm this, is that they're kept separate to help facilitate their own healing and the healing for their victims."

I squint at Reif. "That's an unusually compassionate view. Are you sure you weren't a psychologist in your mortal life?"

He smiles. "No, which is unfortunate. Then I might have an idea of what to do about Jackie. Her pain seems unreachable. That was a brilliant move back there, by the way. I think she really started listening to you once she knew that you were really listening to her."

"I worry about her obsession with getting vengeance. I don't think that's helping her move on."

"Probably not. But neither will dismissing her feelings. So nice work."

"Thanks. And same for you about the Hell thing. It never even occurred to me to ask."

"Just don't tell Jackie I think it's a place where they get help and don't suffer eternal torment."

"Don't worry. If I mention it, it'll be all fire and brimstone, I promise."

Finding Mindi is harder than I expect. The campus has multiple buildings with branching corridors and multiple levels. We have the advantage of not needing to use the doors, so we make faster progress than if we'd had bodies by passing through walls from one room to the next. But it's also easier to get turned around and leave classrooms unchecked.

"Look," I say, pointing to a poster. It's announcing a memorial service for Jackie to be held at the school that weekend. In the center is a large picture of Jackie looking over her shoulder with a wide grin and eyes gleaming with mirth. A Jackie I've never seen.

"Think we should go?" Reif asks.

"They probably won't have a proper funeral for a long time. So yeah, we should go. This might be the closest thing she'll get."

I look at the clock in the hall and realize we'll never finish searching the school before the students are dismissed. We head back to the parking lot, and just as we join Jackie, the bell rings. Students start streaming out of the building, filing to their cars singly and in groups. I keep an eye on the buses as the campus fills with frenetic energy.

Doors slam, kids laugh, horns honk, and the exits clog. A typical day at South Billings High.

"There she is!" I spot Mindi walking to the bus. "There, in the blue jacket with the messenger bag."

"Ah, she's a cutie!" Reif says. "She looks like you."

I elbow him. Of course she doesn't. I was awkward and coltish at that age. Mindi is beautiful.

A boy in a gray hoodie runs up behind her and she turns, grinning. They're too far away to hear their conversation, but her eyes sparkle as he wraps his arm around her shoulder and she leans against him. My smile droops. Too fast. They are moving too fast.

Mindi and her boyfriend move toward the same bus. Is he a neighbor, then? I scan my memory for the families that lived on our street and I can't remember any with boys Mindi's age. Judging by the state of the boy's theater room, they probably don't live anywhere near our neighborhood. Maybe he's going home from school with her. Hours before Richard will be home from work.

I feel a phantom pain in my chest as if my heart wants to race with worry, my breath quickening.

Mindi is a smart girl. She won't let herself get too carried away by the first boy who pays attention to her.

Will she?

My eyes meet Jackie's and shame makes me want to look away. My worries for Mindi are nothing compared to the grief Jackie's mom is feeling. Mindi might make some mistakes and have some regrets, but at least she still has a future. At least those regrets don't include dying too young and never making the most of her amazing potential.

"She seems nice," Jackie says noncommittally.

I can't answer. What can I say to this girl who should

have been there with her friends thinking of nothing scarier than the next science test or research paper? Somehow I feel like I need to apologize.

"Were we ever this young?" Reif says, watching a group of boys piling into an old Chevy with rust lining the seams. "They're just babies." Then he catches Jackie's expression and falls silent as well.

We wait there until the buses pull away from the curb. We wait until the last of the parents file through the pick-up line. We wait until the teachers exit the school one by one and most of the cars in the parking lot are gone.

The driver of the dark green truck never appears.

The sky has gone gray and street lamps have turned on when Jackie finally sighs and jumps off the hood.

"This is stupid," she says and heads back toward where we left the car.

Sixteen

For some reason, we all think we're entitled to a long life. Statistically, almost a third of people die before they reach old age, yet we still see their deaths as premature.

Tragic.

And the younger we are when we die, the more likely we are to look for someone to blame.

For me, it was the doctors. When someone else holds all the cards and then after explaining everything says, "You decide," you can't help but wonder if it's the set-up for a practical joke.

How can I know what treatment is best when I don't even know how to pronounce half the words you just used?

For my friend Jackie, well, let's just say that her anger is more personal. I can tell she must have been a fighter when she was alive.

But when the person or thing you're trying to fight exists

in the mortal world and you do not, that fight gets a lot more complicated.

Jackie refuses to see any more visions.

"It's a waste of time."

She puts on her headphones and closes her eyes, burrowing deeper into a bean bag.

That's fine with me. Looking for her killer isn't doing her any good. Eventually she'll learn that nothing she does here can change the past.

But that would be easier to accept if she had a proper funeral. Instead, a memorial will have to do.

For the four days leading up to the service, Jackie sulks. She sulks on the bean bag. She sulks on my couch. She sulks in the sunshine on the balcony. I suggest going for walks in the park. Reif suggests something a little more adventurous—spelunking in a system of caverns rumored to have an underwater lake. But she brushes us both off and sits for hour after hour with her headphones and a sketchpad.

She's acting like a typical moody teenager, but I know better. She isn't typical. And this isn't moodiness.

On the third day, I return to the Therapy Center.

"Hello, Lorna," Patsy greets me at the front desk. "I assume you've heard that Teresa passed on."

"Yeah, I figured. Pretty exciting." I try to sound happy for her instead of just annoyed at her poor timing.

"Yes, it is. We'll miss her, of course, but it's for the

best. Would you like to set up an appointment with someone else?"

"Actually, I have a friend who needs to see someone. She didn't have a Greeter when she transitioned, and she hasn't had a counselor assigned to her yet. When I talked to Teresa, she said Jackie's case was too complicated and she couldn't recommend anyone. But Jackie really needs to see someone soon. Is there anything you can do?"

Patsy touches the screen mounted to the wall. "Hmm, do you know her last name and when she arrived?"

"Renfro. It's been..." I pause to think. "It's been a couple of weeks."

Patsy focuses on the screen and I know she's found Jackie when her eyes soften and she smiles. "Jackie Renfro is a remarkable girl. She's had a hard time of it, hasn't she?"

"Yeeeah," I say, annoyed at how inadequate that statement is.

"It looks like I might be able to get her in to see someone in...about a month?"

"A month?" I don't bother hiding my dismay. "She's already been waiting for two weeks. That seems really unusual to make her wait so long."

"I'm sorry, Lorna. But I just can't do anything before that."

"Okay, so can I talk to someone else? Is there someone with more authority who can help me?"

"Sure, but she won't be able to do anything either. I have access to the same information she has."

"Then what about *her* boss? Who decides these things anyway?"

Patsy looks at me sympathetically. "Lorna, you've been here long enough to know how things work here. We don't know who makes the rules. We just know what we can and can't do."

"But you must have some idea," I press. "Who trains you?"

"We train our replacements. They'll train their replacements. It's a little less rigid than what you're used to seeing in the mortal world. Ultimately our purpose is to help people pass on. Within that, we've got quite a bit of leeway."

I lean one elbow on the counter. "Okay, so if you've got a lot of leeway, does that mean you can bend some of the restrictions about interacting with the mortal world?"

Patsy shakes her head and laughs. "Well, that's just physics, dear. Can't change that!"

"What if it was necessary for helping someone pass on?" I insist. "What if you had someone who really needed to talk to someone in the mortal world? Could some rules be bent there?"

Patsy's smile fades. "I don't think so, dear. It's just the way things are. You can't interact with the physical world without having a physical body. It's science."

"That's really stupid."

Patsy chuckles indulgently. "I don't know about that. But I've seen this system work over and over again for people like you and me. Trust in it. Now, are you sure you don't want to meet with a new counselor? I could get you in this afternoon if you'd like."

I raise an eyebrow. "You can get me in this afternoon, but Jackie has to wait another month?"

Patsy shrugs. "It's complicated."

The morning of Jackie's memorial, she's ready early and dressed in a black dress with a skirt cut on the bias that fits her waist to perfection, draping past her hips to skim her knees. Her auburn hair is pulled up in a bulky twist and she wears a black hat with a wisp of tulle making a formless veil. She looks like an actress out of a classic Hollywood movie.

"You look gorgeous!" I say, marveling at how the change of clothes seems to age her.

She gives an embarrassed smile, one hand touching her hat. "It's silly, I know. But I've always wanted to wear a hat like this."

"No, it's not silly at all." Immediately I change into a black dress and look at my reflection in the full-length mirror against the wall. "Hmm. I don't pull off black as well as you do."

"It's not the color," Jackie says with a frown. "But that style...it's a bit dated, don't you think?"

I look critically at the matching sweater embroidered with tiny silver roses. "I guess. This was what I wore to my dad's funeral, but that was a long time ago. What would you suggest?"

Jackie grabs my stationery pad. "How about something like this? Timeless. Elegant." She sketches a rough approximation of a sleeveless, fitted shift dress.

"Knee length? It's been years since I've dared. Too many varicose veins."

"What veins?" Jackie says with a laugh. "You don't have blood, remember?"

"Oh right."

Even without the veins, I know there's no way I'll look like her sketch. The rough outline of a model in her drawing clearly didn't have two children and the extra belly flab to show for it. And the lack of sleeves certainly wouldn't accommodate my slug-like arms. But I don't want to hurt Jackie's feelings—it's her memorial service after all—so I imagine myself wearing the dress she drew.

"Whoa," Jackie says admiringly.

"Does it look better than yoga pants?" I say wryly as I turn back to the mirror.

"Just a bit."

"Whoa," I agree, looking at my reflection with awe. Where is my baby pooch? Where are the saggy arms? It's still me, but I look like a younger version of myself. Not only have I shed the ravages of cancer, it seems that I've lost twenty years of pregnancy and stretch marks and stress and sleepless nights. It's like I'm looking at the me that I always felt I was inside, no matter what I saw when I looked in the mirror.

Jackie's grinning face appears over my shoulder. "It's probably good Richard won't be able to see you today. You'd make his girlfriend jealous."

I look at her sharply. "Who told you that?"

"What?"

"Who told you about Richard's girlfriend?"

Jackie's grin falters and she takes a step back. "Sorry. Was it a secret? I asked Reif why you're still here, why you haven't passed on yet."

I put my hands on my hips, the fabric light and smooth beneath my fingers. "And what did Reif say?"

"He said that you've had a hard time accepting that death changes love. He told me that Richard has a girlfriend and you worry that he's stopped loving you, and that makes it hard to let him go."

I feel a flare of annoyance that Reif would have talked about this with Jackie. But I probably would have told her myself if she'd asked. "I know it's healthy, but it's hard to see someone take my place. Death hasn't changed my love for him. It's hard knowing he doesn't feel the same way."

I turn back to my reflection and try to distract myself by testing different shoes. Hoping Jackie will drop it. But a heavy expectation hangs in the room and I know she has more to say.

"I don't know anything about marriage, not really. My dad hasn't been around much, and my mom never seems to have time for men. I've never even had a real boyfriend," she adds shyly. "But I'm sure Richard still loves you. I wonder if for him it's like putting his love for you in a box. It's still there and won't go away, but since it's packed away it also can't grow. Maybe that's the only way he can stand it for you to be gone. And while it's packed away, he can make room to love someone else."

Her words are like sharp claws in my heart, but I

know she means well. I sense her watching me, but I avoid her eyes in the mirror, not wanting to betray my feelings. This is the longest conversation we've had that didn't revolve around her murder.

"I guess he's the lucky one, then," I say, changing my sandal to a shapely pump, then elongating the heel to a length I never would have dared when alive. "He doesn't have to feel guilty about seeing someone else."

"I'm sure he had to work through plenty of guilt, Lorna."

"But it's not the same. Not like it would be for me. I can see him and hear his voice and keep those feelings fresh. I would feel like a vile betrayer if I were to develop feelings for someone else." Just the thought makes my insides twist.

"Maybe that's why Reif doesn't think the visions do you any good."

"What do you mean?"

Jackie adjusts her hat in the mirror, repositioning a pin.

"He thinks the visions make it too hard for you to let go. He says it keeps everything too fresh, that the past makes it too hard to make space for your future."

I want to ask her more, about what sort of future Reif thinks I have, but just then Reif enters the room, startling me with a loud whistle.

"Wow! I was looking for Lorna and Jackie, but I guess I'll take you gorgeous girls instead." He pauses, looking at our expressions. "I'm sorry, am I interrupting? I thought we wanted to get to the memorial early."

"It's fine." I'm glad that I can't blush. "We're ready when you are."

"I was just going to go casual, but that's not going to work now. Give me a sec." He wrinkles his nose, thinking. Instantly his sweater and chinos are replaced by a black tuxedo and tie.

I laugh. "That's a little much, don't you think?"

"Have you seen yourself?" he asks incredulously.

I duck my head, pleased but embarrassed. "You like it then? Jackie came up with it."

"She's got great taste. You look amazing."

I want to ask him if he thinks I look younger than when he first met me, but it's not a conversation I want to have in front of Jackie.

Instead, I surreptitiously shoot glances at him as he heads to open the door for us. Does he look younger than before? Maybe. It's been months since he lost the hard, wrinkled look of an alcoholic. His skin is unblemished and I find myself wondering what his aftershave used to smell like.

Probably expensive.

And irresistible.

He holds open the door for "the most beautiful dead ladies he'd ever seen," and Jackie laughs. He kisses her on the cheek as she passes, and she cries out at the sting, holding her cheek in playful indignation. As I pass, he doesn't touch me, but the look in his eyes stirs something in my chest. Something like longing. For once I don't want to push it away.

"Mrs. Preston, may I escort you to the illustrious hall of competitive athletic exhibition?"

I pause a beat, distracted by the intensity of his blue eyes. "Oh, the gym? Um, sure."

He offers me his arm and I take it, trying to pretend that instead of the dissonant shock where we touch, I can feel the weight and warmth of his arm under my hand.

Seventeen

The high school parking lot is packed. Without speaking, we all pause for a moment before walking in. I scan the lot for the dark green truck. It isn't there.

"I'll check again later," Reif offers. "Let's get you inside."

It's nice to show up early for your own funeral service. Most people prefer it so they can see the behind-the-scenes set-up and revel in each guest as they arrive.

There will be no reveling at Jackie's memorial. We're an hour early and the gym is already almost half full. The first two rows of metal chairs are roped off. "Reserved for family." Jackie has only talked about her mom. I wonder who else will be sitting in those chairs.

A stage has been erected on the far end of the basketball court, festooned with gorgeous floral arrangements. A string quintet made up of teenagers dressed in concert black plays in the corner under a spotlight, conducted by a thin man with a receding hairline who stoops over his music stand.

Gentle music notwithstanding, the noise level in the echoing gym is high as people greet each other and offer hugs and tissues. Chairs squeak and babies cry, and the quintet plays on. A large screen hangs above the stage and photos of a young Jackie flash above our heads. Jackie as a fat baby grinning as she chews on her toes. Jackie on the first day of kindergarten. Jackie riding a bike. Jackie in a tutu. Jackie blowing bubbles that shimmer in the sun against a bright blue sky.

"Ugh." Jackie grimaces. "I can't believe they did a slideshow. How embarrassing."

"It's sweet," Reif says.

"I don't even know most of these people. I only moved here last year. They just came to gawk. Like grief vampires," she says derisively.

She has a point. Some of the teenagers jostling for the closer seats look like they're more concerned about adopting a properly tragic face than actually feeling anything for the victim. And they aren't the only ones. Some of the adults with long faces and wet eyes get dark glances from Jackie, and I gather that they are total strangers. On the other hand, Vince and Ray hold back, taking their seats a good distance from the stage as if afraid someone might notice them.

But I understand the huge turnout and the emotion from total strangers. "Whenever someone young dies tragically like this, the whole community feels profoundly affected. Even if we don't know them personally, we feel it deeply. It touches on our worst fears. We think of our own kids and try to understand what it would be like to be in your mom's shoes."

"I don't want anyone to understand," Jackie says grumpily.

I don't say any more.

When my family enters the gym, dressed in clothes they would normally wear going out to eat at a nice restaurant, I want to go to them. But then I see the woman trailing behind them, and how Richard stops to let her into the row to sit with the kids, and my enthusiasm plummets.

Richard's girlfriend is older than I expected, her face creased with laugh lines around the eyes. She has light brown hair but her complexion hints that it may have once been blond before darkening with age. I look at her critically and am begrudgingly pleased to see that she is neither too pretty nor too homely. She looks both intelligent and compassionate, just as I would hope for Richard. But as she reaches out and pats Mindi's leg affectionately and smiles at Richard as he puts his arm around her, I can't help but feel a surge of distaste.

Reif watches my expression and leans in close. "Hey, they're still your family. She's not stealing them from you. She's just taking care of them while you're gone."

I grunt and turn away.

As the room fills, Reif suggests we take some seats. We sit on the front row of chairs, and I'm glad that we don't have to feel the cold metal pressing into our skin the way it does for the living.

"There's my mom!" Jackie jumps up.

Mrs. Renfro enters through an interior door, escorted

by two tall men in suits. A hush falls over the crowd and they stand in a chorus of scraping chairs.

"Uncle James! And Uncle Darryl! They came all the way from Seattle? And there's Aunt Meg and Aunt Jenny. Oh!" Her hands fly to her mouth as half a dozen children follow in behind the adults, dressed in black, their faces somber.

"This is your family?" I ask.

She nods, too affected to speak.

Her cousins pass so close we could have reached out and touched them. "Hi guys," she calls softly with a little wave. "Thanks for coming. Thanks for taking care of my mom. Give her lots of hugs from me."

The crowd stands in near silence. The only sound comes from the string quintet, a minor piece that I briefly wonder if Reif recognizes. Once Jackie's mom sits, a man on the stage rises and approaches the podium. The music ceases. He's dressed in black with the tell-tale white collar of a pastor. He adjusts the microphone and it sounds like scratching a vinyl record.

"Please be seated." His voice echoes around the room. "On behalf of the Renfro family, I thank you for coming today to honor the life of a truly extraordinary young woman."

"That's Reverend Markham," Jackie mutters. "He's nice enough, I guess. Mom likes him."

"You don't?"

She shrugs. "He always used to look at me like he thought I was up to no good. I don't like it when adults do that."

"I always figure that adults who think the worst of

teenagers were the worst kind of teenagers themselves." Reif's observation draws a smirk from Jackie.

Reverend Markham asks for a moment of silence as everyone ponders the great loss the community of Billings has experienced.

"The community of Billings wouldn't even know who I was if I hadn't been murdered," Jackie mutters, folding her arms.

"That may be true, but that doesn't make you any less special. They're just focusing on the wrong reason," I say.

"These poor mortals," Reif adds. "Death doesn't define us nearly as much as they think it does. There's so much more left to look forward to."

"Careful, Reif," I say. "That sounds suspiciously like someone who's preparing to pass on."

He winks at me. But I'm more than a little disturbed by the brightness of his eyes. They seem like they almost see right through me.

What will I do if Reif passes on before me? I've never considered that it might happen, but he's been making me nervous these past few days. Ultimately it's a good thing, I know. But I feel a keen stab of loneliness at the thought.

Reverend Markham's remarks continue in a predictable manner. He speaks of the community's need for each other during this hard time. He speaks of how there was always something special about Jackie and how he knew she'd been destined for great things. Jackie snorts softly at that. He speaks of the need to strengthen Jackie's mom—Brenda is her name—and be good Christians to her. He speaks of holding our own loved ones close and cherishing each other. Many eyes are wet, and further down the row where Jackie's family sits, hands reach for each other.

Jackie's nose wrinkles with disdain.

"You don't feel loved?" I ask with a smile. "Most people don't get this much attention when they die."

"I don't like attention."

After Reverend Markham speaks, we hear from the principal and two other teachers. When Joy Sanders comes to the podium, Jackie stills. For the first time since the meeting started, she listens closely to every word. Joy speaks with a tremor in her voice, as if it won't take much to push her over the edge into hysteria. But she holds it together, speaking fondly of her first impressions of Jackie and how she came to appreciate her as a reliable student who was always willing to try something new and take on a challenge.

When she relates a story about how Jackie offered to take over the after-school yearbook meetings for two weeks while Joy was out with a family health crisis, and how Joy returned to find that the staff was more productive than ever during that time, I find myself wishing I had known Jackie then. The Jackie I know is bitter and angry and afraid. It makes me sad to think I missed the best parts of her by not knowing her when she was alive.

A group of students sing a cheesy country song about saying goodbye to our loved ones and how they live on in our hearts. I expect Jackie to scoff at it, but she listens with eyes wide and luminescent. I suspect they would be filled with tears if it were possible. Either Joy's words or the music has touched her in some way. Softened her.

As the last chords of the song die away, Uncle James rises from his seat and goes to the stage. He gives a brief synopsis of Jackie's life. Her childhood in Seattle. How her parents' divorce brought out her more creative side through poetry and songwriting. He speaks of her dreams to go to college and be a journalist. He talks about how she cared deeply about troubling things going on in the world and was dedicated to making a difference.

Jackie shifts next to me. "It's like he's talking about a different person."

"You didn't have those dreams?"

"No, I did. It's just that...never mind."

"I felt that way at my funeral too. It's weird to hear other people's perceptions of you."

"It's not just that," Jackie says sadly. "It's like I forgot who I was. Like he took that from me too."

I reach for her hand and squeeze, sending a little jolt. She's getting more comfortable with that sort of contact now and doesn't immediately pull her hand away.

When Uncle Darryl stands up, Reif leans over. "I'm going to go check the parking lot. Just to be sure."

He doesn't return for some time, so it's only Jackie and I there when her mom stands and approaches to the microphone. I draw in a quick breath, surprised that she would dare speak to this intimidating crowd when her heart has to be breaking. Darryl embraces her as he returns to his seat, and Brenda shrinks a little into his arms. But after he releases her, she walks straight and tall to the podium. When she speaks, her voice is pinched with emotion.

"My heart is full seeing so many of you coming out today to express love for my little girl. I know most of you don't know me, and maybe you didn't even know her. But I feel your love and support and am grateful for it. Billings has only been our home for a little while, but it will always be home now. We've been bound together in our grief.

"I appreciate Chief Datillo coming out here today." Brenda nods to the police chief sitting near the front. "She and her officers have been working tirelessly to find the person who took my Jackie from me. I appreciate their dedication and sensitivity, and I know that someday I will see justice done."

She pauses for a moment, twisting a white handkerchief in her hand. When she resumes, her voice is stronger, like she's reached the real point of her message.

"But I know Jackie wouldn't want us to waste our lives in grieving. If she were here, I'm sure she would tell us to take this pain and use it to help each other. She would tell us to put our strength into looking out for those who are less fortunate than we are. Those who live in fear and violence all the time. She would tell us to be kinder to each other. To laugh more. To love more. And not to let another day pass wasted in anger or hate or pining for what can't be. She would tell us to embrace life and live it fully. She would tell us that the most important risks we can ever take in this life are to love and forgive. So, Jackie, if you can hear me," her voice cracks a little and she takes an anchoring breath, "I'm here to tell you that in the sixteen years I was so lucky to be your mom, I listened. And I'm going to live the rest of my life the way you would have if you were here."

The feeling in the room is as if a bright light has pierced through a dark fog. Heads nod, faces are dry and smiling.

"Wow," I say as Brenda returns to her seat. "Your mom is pretty incredible."

"Yeah she is." It's little more than a whisper.

Mrs. Renfro's progress to her chair is interrupted by Jackie's Aunt Meg standing to hug her. Jackie waits until they're finished and her mother is seated before standing and walking to her. She reaches out, bending slightly to place one hand on her mother's cheek. Brenda looks right through her to the stage where Reverend Markham is standing again to offer closing remarks. I wish with all my heart that Brenda could see her daughter there. Beautiful and strong and her essence still alive.

"I love you, Mom," Jackie says fiercely, her voice thick with emotion. "I miss you so much."

Brenda doesn't react.

After a long moment staring into her face, Jackie drops her hand and turns away. So she doesn't see, as I do, her mother reach up to gently brush her cheek where Jackie's hand just rested.

Eighteen

Death Therapy is an awkward term, but it really sums up the work that goes on here. Even natural causes of death can still be traumatic and victims need help sorting out their complicated feelings. Grief over what they've lost. Guilt about leaving loved ones behind. Shame over poor choices that hastened it.

I have a friend who spent much of his mortal life as an alcoholic. It ruined his marriage and his career, and eventually cost him his life when he passed out while soaking in a tub. I don't know if he was more appalled that he drowned like that or that it was almost a week before anyone missed him enough to check up on him.

The first month was hard, but being in this place has been so good for him. I would have thought he would have passed on long before now, but he must have something keeping him behind. Something that he won't talk to me about. It makes me sad because I thought he trusted me more than that. But maybe when he finally feels like he can talk *about it, that will be his last act of letting go and then he'll pass on.*

Is it selfish of me to hope it's not too soon?

~

"Are you ready to go, Jacks?" Reif says as he plops down on a bean bag next to her.

She doesn't respond. She's been writing in a notebook all afternoon with earbuds in, occasionally humming along with her music.

He pats her knee and she looks up. "I'm ready when you are."

"Where are you going?" I ask, turning over the letter I'm working on.

"I thought we'd go back to the high school to see if we could track down the owner of that truck."

"I don't want to go," Jackie says, pulling out her earbuds.

I look at her in surprise. "What's up?"

Jackie closes her notebook with a sigh. She's sporting a nose ring at the moment. A recent addition. "Mom wouldn't let me get one when I was alive," she'd explained with a shrug when I noticed it.

Now she looks up at me with a thoughtful expression in her brown eyes. "I've been thinking a lot about what my mom said at the memorial. The person she described, that's who I was before. But that's not who I've been since this happened."

"So it's changed you. That's okay. It was a traumatic—"

"Yeah, but I don't want it to change me that way. I want to be that person that she described. I want to be the one who can look past her own pain and be aware of the people around her. I want to be the kind of person who fights for healing and hope, not vengeance and hatred."

Reif leans forward, resting his elbows on his knees. "Do you think that leaving this investigation alone will do that for you?"

"Investigation?" Jackie scoffs. "What sort of investigation is this anyway? We can't access any real evidence. We can't talk to people and ask them questions. Even visiting my memories was pointless. We're just a bunch of ghosts blindly bouncing around Billings and hoping something turns up."

"That's too bad," Reif says with a smirk. "I was thinking of starting a true crime television series, afterlife edition."

Jackie's lips quirk in a reluctant smile. "Yeah, well, I hope you had more success on your real life cases than you've had on mine."

"Actually..." He cracks his knuckles noiselessly. "To be honest, I didn't have any real life cases."

"Oh?" I perk up. "Do tell, Reif. You mean to say you weren't a Portland homicide detective?"

"Nah."

"You weren't?" Jackie sounds disappointed. "I thought for sure..."

"Well, I had some connections," Reif says. "I tried to be really thorough in my research."

"Research?"

"I was a writer. Crime thrillers, that sort of thing."

"Seriously?" I laugh and Jackie drops her notebook in surprise.

"You don't have to laugh about it!"

"Were you any good?"

"Pretty good, yeah. You ever hear of Mason Watts?"

"Whatever, Reif."

"No really, he's mine."

I swivel in my chair and peer at him, trying to detect a lie. The characteristic sparkle in his eyes is gone. If anything, he seems embarrassed.

That alone tells me it's true.

"No. Way." Awe washes over me. "*You* are Gerald Houston?"

"Guilty as charged. That was my pen name."

"I can't believe it. Really?"

"So you've heard of me?"

"I haven't," Jackie say, leaning forward. "Who's Gerald Houston?"

"He's a big time author. Like, really big." I stare, trying to reconcile affable Reif with the bestselling author whose books lined our bookshelves. "I can't believe it. Richard loves you. I mean, looooves you. I think we own every book you've ever written."

"Well, thanks for that. Mason was my bread-and-butter series. But to be honest, I was getting bored with him at the end. I was considering killing him off but hadn't quite figured out how to do it. And then...well, you know the rest. I ended up here and Mason lived forever."

Realization dawns.

"I remember now! Richard was so ticked when you died. It put him in a funk for days! One of the most boring visions I ever visited. It must have been right around the time I met you, but I never put it together that I'd just met the real Gerald-freaking-Houston. Man, I wish I could tell him now! 'Honey, you'll never guess who my best friend is!'"

Jackie cocks her head at Reif. "Why didn't you tell us? Why keep it a secret all this time?"

"Because I didn't want to have this conversation." He passes a hand through his hair, looking as if he wishes he could take it back. "I liked being plain old Reif Thursby. No reputation to live up to. No expectations to disappoint. All that success didn't make my life any easier. Didn't convince my wife to stay with me."

"Her loss, man. I can't even believe it. Gerald Houston all this time! I confess I only read one of your books. I can't remember the name. Something about a jury...and the real murderer is actually the judge or something?"

"*Hung Jury*?"

"Yeah, that must have been it. It was a bit dark for my taste, though. I couldn't do any more after that. But Richard, he was a big fan. Pretty much every Christmas would include your latest Mason Watts and then we wouldn't see him for two days while he devoured it."

"I'm glad I could do my part to come between you and Dicky on special occasions."

I burst out a short laugh. "Don't say that, Reif!"

"Why not? What you remember most about my life's work is that it interrupted your holiday. Not exactly something to be proud of. And sadly, that's about all I can muster at this point," Reif says grimly.

"Give yourself some credit," I protest. "Your books brought Richard a lot of joy, and that means something. Giving someone a way to escape the darkness once in a while is a huge gift. And I'm betting millions of other readers would agree. Maybe your life was hard, but at least you left your mark on the world. That's more than I can say."

"Or me," Jackie says.

That quells my humor. Poor Jackie will go down in history as the victim of a horrible crime and that's all the world will remember her for. She'll never have a chance to make her mark the way she wanted.

"What would you have liked to do if you had lived, Jackie?" Reif asks, seizing the chance to change the subject. "Your story isn't over yet, you know."

"What do you mean?"

"It's true," I say, remembering Reif's words to me. "The fact that we die with all our memories and hopes and dreams intactmeans that we must use them after we pass on. I'll bet we have opportunities that we've never imagined. What do you think you would like to do if you could do anything?"

Jackie picks at her lower lip thoughtfully. "I...I don't know. I would have liked to go to college, but I hadn't decided what I wanted to do after that."

"What did you want to study? Journalism?"

"Nah." She grimaces. "I used to. But for the past few months I'd been thinking of doing something a little more meaningful. I really wanted to change things, not just talk about it."

"What kind of things?"

Her eyes brighten as she lists a few. "Poverty. Human trafficking. Did you know that there are thirty million victims of human trafficking around the world, lots of them right here in the United States? I learned about it in school and it blew me away. Do you think I'd be able to do something about that when I pass on? Help all those people?"

"Yes," Reif says with certainty. "I absolutely think so."

"I would like that," she says. "I would like that a lot."

Her expression is so hopeful that I don't contradict Reif, but I wonder how he can be so certain. I catch his eye and shoot him a questioning look. He raises an eyebrow in return as if to say he's standing his ground. And for a moment, just a brief moment, I feel a certainty wash over me that he's right.

It passes and is replaced with skepticism, but in that brief moment I think I see a little sheen pass over Reif's face.

That conversation marks a change for Jackie. She peppers both of us with questions about what we know about passing on. She searches out the teenage girls she met at the Arrival plaza and learns as much as she can from them. They don't know much, but making friends her own age brings out a side of her I haven't seen before. She experiments with her image, moving her piercing to different locations, adding tattoos, and changing her hair on an almost daily basis—easy enough to do with a thought.

In the evenings, she dances to hip hop or sits for hours with her journal, scribbling away with a distant look in her eye.

"I'm done with being stuck," Jackie says. "I want to own my life, whatever that looks like."

"Good for you. This is your story to write, no one else's." I find myself talking like Teresa sometimes and missing my family less when I do. The pain is replaced with hope for good things still to come.

It's also a turning point for me.

"I want to be like Jackie," I tell Reif a few days later.

We're sitting against a large ash tree on the bank of a crystal clear river. The gentle burbling of the water running over the rocks sounds genuine enough, but I miss the smell of the grass and the cool breeze that should be wafting toward us from the river. Usually missing those details doesn't bother me in this world, but today I want more.

"I've realized that I've put my life on hold all this time," I say. "It's kind of a waste."

"You're just now realizing that?" Reif's voice is a low murmur, his tone relaxed and soothing.

"I don't just mean here. I mean..." I hesitate to say what I'm thinking. "Devoting myself to Richard and the kids meant I didn't always pay attention to who Lorna was. Those were such great years and I don't have any regrets. But now I realize that with all the people I was taking care of, sometimes I forgot to take care of me. I had my job, and that was fine. But I didn't care deeply about it. It was something I just fell into. Listening to Jackie reminds me that I was once passionate about issues like she is. I once had dreams of things I wanted to accomplish. But I let my dreams get replaced by Richard's dreams and Mindi's dreams and even Alex's dreams."

I'm relieved they can't hear me now. Am I being disloyal? I know Reif won't judge me, but I try to clarify my feelings for my own sake.

"I wouldn't change anything exactly," I add, "except that I wish I had paid a little more attention to what comes after. Because even before I knew that I wouldn't live to see age forty, I always knew that there would come a day when Mindi and Alex would be gone and not need me so much. It would have been nice if when that day came I wasn't wondering what to do with myself."

Reif shifts next to me, his shoulder pressing against mine. At moments like this, I can almost imagine that we have bodies again and I can feel him properly instead of the dissonant humming sensation that accompanies non-corporeal beings touching. Having him here is comforting in a familiar way that fills me with yearning.

"'After' came a little sooner for us both than we expected, didn't it?" he says.

"Yeah, but it doesn't seem like such a tragedy anymore. It just is. It was only a tragedy before, in that life. But in the 'after', it can just be a little footnote as I move on to something else. Maybe even something better. I've been told it so many times; I've even told other people the same thing. But this is the first time I've believed it."

I draw my knees up to my chest and wrap my arms around them.

Reif watches me beneath half-lidded eyes. "So, what do you want to do in your 'after?'"

"I don't know. But it's kind of exciting to have possibilities, don't you think?"

"I do. I really do."

We sit there in silence for a long while, watching the white clouds glowing with sunshine against a brilliant autumn sky. Leaves carpet the ground around us, leaving the branches overhead sparse and empty.

"I'm going to the Vision Station," I announce.

"Uh oh."

"No, this is good. I'm ready to say goodbye. *Really* say goodbye."

I stand and brush off my backside where I'd been sitting. A remembered habit. Reif jumps up after me.

"Are you sure?"

I can sense his excitement and smile. "Yes, I'm sure. It feels right. More right than it's ever felt before. I'm ready."

Again, Reif gives me that look. Again, his eyes are so bright that I can almost see them glowing with expectation. I feel a flutter of excitement, but also nervousness. If he passes on before me, I hope I'll follow soon. This is the first time that hope doesn't seem like an idle wish.

Nineteen

Dearest Richard,

I thought I already said goodbye to you. I know you said your goodbyes to me three years ago. But I didn't realize that letting you go would be so hard. That I would still be hanging on, clinging to you like I couldn't survive without you. It seems ironic now, since I'm the one who left you in the first place.

You've learned to move on. At first I was angry. I felt betrayed. But I see now that as long as death keeps us apart, it's for the best. Moving on is the best thing for you, for the kids, and even for me. I've been stuck for three years, unable to move on or let go. I thought I was happy, but really I was just trapped. I've finally realized that I don't want that. And I don't want it for you either.

Someday I will see you again, and I'm sure I'll love you just as much then as I did the day I died. But in the meantime, I have other things to do. There's more to come for me. I don't know what, but instead of feeling resentful, I'm excited. I'll miss you and Mindi and Alex always. But there are other people who need me. Other people to love.

I pause, considering what I just wrote. I think about how happy Richard seems with his new girlfriend. I think about what Reif said as we watched them together, how she's taking care of my family while I'm gone.

Don't worry that I'll forget you. That's impossible, just as I know you'll never forget me even as you're making a new life with her. I don't know what the future will bring. I don't know how long it will be before I see you again. But in the meantime, you'll be happy to know that I have someone else taking care of me.

I finish the letter I'll never send, and my fingers shimmer as I fold it.

I didn't visit the Vision Station last week, so I have a full hour of credit to use. That should be enough. No sense drawing this out longer than I need to. I just want to see them all one last time.

 I join my family in the kitchen where Richard is looking for his keys and Alex is pouring himself a glass of milk.

 Mindi comes into the room breathlessly, dressed in a

wide-necked, off-the-shoulder sweatshirt and tight jeggings.

Richard frowns at her. "I'm not sure about that shirt. Don't you have something you can wear under it?"

"It's fine, Dad," Mindi huffs. "Don't be so old."

He clears his throat and shoots her a look over his glasses. "I *am* old. That's why I can afford to pay for your clothes, and you're not leaving the house only wearing half of them. I'm not taking you anywhere until you change. Or that shirt is going in the trash and I'm buying you turtlenecks."

"Dad! I told Kyle I would be there by now!"

"Then you'd better find something else quick."

Mindi groans, but she turns around and goes back up the stairs.

"Nicely done, Richard," I mutter with a smile.

When Mindi returns, she's still in the same sweatshirt, but a wide tank top covers most of her shoulder. Richard nods his approval.

"Better. And Kyle will bring you home by ten?"

"But Dad, it's not a school night. Tomorrow is Thanksgiving. It's practically a weekend."

Now it's Richard's turn to sigh. "You're almost seventeen. All right. Midnight. But if anything comes up and you feel even a little bit uncomfortable, text me and I'll drop everything and come get you."

"Yeah, yeah, got it." Mindi tosses the words over her shoulder as she runs toward the garage.

Richard looks at Alex. "You're not going to grow up that fast, are you?"

Alex shrugs noncommittally.

"I know. Too late. All right, Alex, I'll be back in a bit. You'll be ready to go to the Swansons' when I get back?"

He doesn't wait for an answer before following after Mindi.

As soon as Richard is gone, Alex grabs his glass of milk and a package of cookies and takes them both into the living room, something I'm pretty sure Richard would frown on. He plops on the couch and grabs the remote. I wonder briefly if I should end the vision so I don't spend my last moments with Alex watching him watch TV. But there's something about it that reminds me of coming to check on him at night when he was little, those moments lingering in the doorway watching him sleep.

I mentally trace his perfect profile and marvel at how much it'll change in the next few years as he grows into a man. For a moment I think about missing those years and my confidence in my decision flickers momentarily. But there will always be the next thing. There will always be reasons to postpone saying goodbye. High school graduation, college, weddings, grandbabies...there will always be something more I don't want to miss. If this is the last image of my son to take with me, it's as good as any.

"I love you so much, Alex," I say. "I hope you'll always know that. And if your dad gets married again, I hope you will appreciate her and always know that I loved you first."

Alex sits blankly, his eyes tracking the action on the screen. I wish there was some way he could know that I'm here.

I think of that moment at Jackie's memorial when it seemed like Jackie's mom sensed her presence. I haven't talked to Jackie or Reif about what I saw. I can't be sure it's what I thought and Jackie is making such great progress that I don't want to derail her from passing on.

But now I stand in front of Alex and place my hands on his cheeks as Jackie did to her mom. I feel nothing. As far as I'm concerned, I'm just holding my hands in the air.

"I love you so much," I repeat, pouring my heart into the words. "I hope you know that. I hope you will always know that."

He doesn't react. I wait, holding my hands still in case it takes time to soak in or something.

Nothing.

I'm surprised to hear the door to the garage and discover that Richard has returned. I've been staring into Alex's face for longer than I realized. When I release him, there is still no reaction.

"You ready to go?" Richard asks as he tosses his keys onto the table. He's dressed like he's ready to go out, and for a moment I imagine I can smell his aftershave and wonder if it's still the same one he used when I was alive.

"Yeah, just about," Alex says. He heads toward the stairs, his eyes still fixed on the TV.

"It's not like you haven't seen this episode before," Richard says. "You can finish it when you get back."

With Alex gone, Richard pulls out his phone and thumbs through his apps.

"Hey, Rich," I say, knowing he can't hear me. "I just wanted to let you know that I'm getting ready to pass on.

I'm glad you're moving on too. I wasn't at first, but I understand that it's a sign of healing. I just didn't expect my healing would take so long. But I'm in a good place now, and I think it'll be soon."

He smiles at something on his screen, the light illuminating his face. I feel foolish. After so many years of holding on, I have no idea how to say goodbye.

"I guess it's a little silly to be talking to you like this, since you can't even hear me. But I wanted to say that I'm happy for you. And I think I'm going to be happy too. Happier than I expected."

Alex shuffles into the room and Richard clicks off his phone.

"You ready? I told Sandra I'd pick you up at ten."

I stand in the living room alone as they move down the hallway toward the garage.

With one last heavy sigh, I return to the Vision car.

"You have twenty-five minutes remaining in your Vision credit," the voice informs me as soon as the doors close.

"Can you take me straight to Mindi? I didn't get to properly say goodbye and would like to finish my last minutes with her."

It doesn't take long to reach her. When the car door opens, I find myself back in the plush theater room. There isn't a movie on this time. Mindi sits on a leather reclining sofa, Kyle's head in her lap. She's fingering his tousled blond hair. I try to push away the instant feeling of dislike that comes over me. It's normal to feel protective about her relationship with this boy, but that doesn't mean he's actually a bad kid. It probably isn't fair to judge him so harshly just because my daughter likes him.

But still, I wish he wasn't here for my last moments with Mindi.

They're chatting with each other in low voices.

"It's not like they're getting married or anything," Kyle says as I step close enough to hear.

"I know, but what if they do? It's just…I mean, it was hard enough to get used to living without Mom. Trying to get used to a stranger in her place would make things all weird again."

"But you like her, right?"

"Sure. It's nothing against her. She's different from my mom. And that's okay. It would probably be harder if she was too much the same. But I thought we were doing fine just the three of us, and now it's all different."

"Maybe you need to tell her that it's not her job to replace your mother. If she's as great as your dad thinks she is, she'll understand."

"Yeah, maybe."

My esteem for Kyle rises slightly. Maybe I judged him unfairly. I should have known that Mindi is more discerning than that.

In the silence that follows, I sit on the couch opposite them.

"I know you can't hear me, Mindi," I begin. "You'd probably be mortified to know that I'm here, so I guess it's good you can't. But I wanted to say goodbye. This is the last time I'm going to come and watch you, to see how you're growing and progressing. I'll miss you so much, and I wanted to take one last time to tell you that I love you and am so proud of you."

Kyle takes Mindi's hand and gingerly kisses her fingertips. She beams at him.

I find I've run out of things to say.

"Well, I guess that's it, then. I hope you have the most amazing life, Mindi, and always know how special you are."

"Oh!" Mindi cries out.

For a second I think she's heard me and I lean forward with excitement. But she's looking out the large, uncovered window behind me.

"It's snowing!" Mindi cries.

She jumps off the couch with a "hey!" from Kyle as she unceremoniously dumps his head on the cushion.

"Look! It's so pretty!"

Mindi stands at the window, looking at the white flakes coming down against the dusky sky.

Kyle approaches her from behind and wraps his arms around her waist. "Yeah, she is," he says meaningfully. She elbows him playfully, but lets him pull her close.

Does this kid have parents? Siblings? Now would be a great time for someone to come bursting unexpectedly into the room.

I step up next to them, feeling like an inadequate chaperone, and watch the heavy flakes falling from the sky. The air is thick with them, but they haven't yet started sticking to the pavement or the vehicles parked in the driveway.

All at once, the peaceful ember I've been feeling for

the past few days turns cold. For there on the driveway, parked next to a white Lexus, is a dark pickup truck with a shell and extended cab.

Without thinking, I press my face against the window to get a better look and my face instantly passes through it. The rest of my body follows and I jump down to the grass below. The massive house is well-lit, and lamp posts line the driveway. I approach the truck with a heavy sense of dread knotting my stomach. Rounding the back of the truck, I see it right where I expect; the sticky pattern of decal residue hinting at the old logo of the Rimrock Country Club.

In a panic, I run back into the house and upstairs to the waiting car.

"You have eight minutes remaining on your Vision credit."

I curse under my breath. Eight minutes isn't nearly enough.

Twenty

I find Reif watching the new Arrivals, a look of contentment on his face. His face almost glows with it.

"Reif!" I call desperately as I run to him.

"Lorna? What's wrong?" He turns to me, his brow drawn in sudden concern.

"Mindi's boyfriend Kyle. He killed Jackie."

The light in his eyes dies. "How do you know?"

"It's his truck. I found the truck. I was saying goodbye to Mindi and his truck was there in the driveway. We have to help her."

Reif swears and scans the park. In our world, the sun is just beginning to set, the wisps of clouds painted a brilliant fuschia and coral. "Let's find Jackie. She needs to know."

I feel a surge of gratitude that he isn't dismissing me. That he isn't trying to talk me into letting it go with a "we can't stop the bad things that happen to people we love" speech.

Instead, we run through the park searching for Jackie. We find her sitting on a wooden bridge over a creek, framing up views with her fingers like a photographer framing up camera shots.

"Jackie!" Reif's voice carries louder than mine.

She looks up and drops her hands.

We're upon her in a moment.

"I found your killer," I say.

She blinks.

"He was a student at your high school. And he's dating my daughter."

"No way." She scrambles to her feet.

"I'm sorry, I know you've been trying to let this all go. But I need your help."

"My help? What can I do to help?"

"You did something at your memorial. I don't think you even know you did, but somehow your mom felt you there."

Jackie narrows her eyes skeptically. "What are you talking about? She didn't feel anything."

"I know you think she didn't. But after you turned away, I saw her touch her cheek where you'd been touching her face. I think she felt something."

Jackie's lips part. Reif frowns, and I feel a sting of guilt.

"I'm sorry I didn't say anything. I wasn't sure that what I saw was real. And then you decided to let go and move on, and it didn't seem important anymore. I didn't want to do anything to disrupt your healing, especially if

I was wrong."

"What if you're wrong now?"

"I'll take that chance. So far you're the only one I've heard of who's affected the physical world in any way. You're the only hope I have to help Mindi. Can you tell me what you did? How you did it?"

Jackie stalks away. "I can't believe you didn't tell me. I could have gone to the police."

"Now you can! And now you can give them a name and an address! But first I need your help."

"Please, Jackie," Reif says. "Think about everything that you did in that moment."

She stops and looks back at us, her arms crossed in indignation. "Just what you saw. I touched her face and told her I loved her. But she didn't see me or hear me."

"Maybe not, but I do think she felt you. Can you remember feeling anything unusual? Or thinking anything specific?"

Jackie shakes her head. "I just thought about how much I loved her and wanted her to be happy. I didn't feel anything weird or—Actually, that's not true."

"What? What did you feel?"

"Cold. I didn't think much of it at the time, but I do remember almost feeling cold. But not really, more like a memory of what cold used to feel like. I didn't think it was a big deal because it was so short and went away. I forgot it happened until now."

I nod excitedly. "That's a place to start. Thank you!"

"Wait!" Reif calls. "Where are you going?"

"I've got to get a message through to her somehow. Take Jackie to the police station. See if there's some way to get a message to them. I've got to warn Mindi."

"We can't go to the police station without you. It's your friend who works there, remember?"

"Right." I stop. What will keep Mindi safe? Getting a message through to her or telling the police who Jackie's killer was? But I can't even think about anything else while Mindi is there with Kyle. "Sorry, I've got to do this first. Sorry, Jackie. And Reif, I've only got eight minutes left on my Vision credits. Can I use some of yours?"

Reif doesn't hesitate. "Of course."

Together we race back to the Vision Station. While Reif handles the transaction to transfer credits to my name, I bounce on the balls of my feet, jittery with impatience.

I've always thought the Vision cars were supersonic fast, but today it seems to crawl. How long did it take to find Reif and Jackie? How much time passed for Mindi while I was gone?

Reif and Jackie stand next to me in the car. I didn't ask them to come, but I'm glad they're there.

"Not sure if this makes a difference, but he probably won't hurt her," Reif says as we watch the lights flashing out the car. "At least not tonight when Richard knows where she is. If something happens to her, the boyfriend will be the first one the police suspect. And once they see that truck—"

"Yeah, but that doesn't exactly help," I answer. "It would still be too late for Mindi. And here I've been trying to think the best of him. Thinking I was just being overprotective. Turns out he's just a football thug with perverted power issues."

"Football? He's a big kid then?"

"Big compared to Mindi. She wouldn't have a chance —" I choke off, dread making it hard to speak. Gone is the peace and reassurance I felt earlier in the day. How could I have thought I was ready to pass on? Now that warmth and hope is gone, replaced with cold, hard fear.

The car delivers us to the backyard of Kyle's house. Snow is now sticking to the grass, forming a layer an inch thick. Mindi and Kyle sit on a wooden porch swing, bundled in a blanket.

Mindi's eyes shine and her cheeks are pink with cold.

As I did with Alex, I stand before Mindi, my hands on either side of her face.

"Mindi," I say firmly. "Mindi, you must listen to me. This boy is dangerous. Mindi, can you hear me? I need you to listen."

She tilts her head and laughs as Kyle kisses her cheek. I swipe at his face, but my hand passes right through him.

"Why isn't it working?" I ask in despair, looking at Reif. He shrugs helplessly.

"Mindi, please. Listen to me. I'm your mom. I love you more than anyone. Please, just listen. I need you to go home and never see this boy again. He's done terrible things. You need to stay far away from him."

I glance at Jackie. She's staring into the house, unwilling to even look at her killer.

"Jackie, please help me. I don't know what to do."

She turns away as if in a daze. "I don't know either. I'm sorry, Lorna. I don't know what I did."

"Alright, let's think about this," Reif says, pacing on the flagstone patio. "You both share the same blood. Close relationship. Jackie was focused and intent—"

"So am I!" I protest.

Reif stops pacing. "Yes, but she isn't."

"What?" Jackie asks.

"When your mom felt you, she'd been thinking of you. And not just casually. She had just been talking *to* you in her speech at the memorial. She was just as focused and intent as you were."

I look at Mindi and my hope plummets. "But she's not thinking of me at all."

We watch Mindi and Kyle giggling together on the swing. I seethe with hatred for the boy. How could such a monster pretend to be so normal?

"What can I do?" I moan. "How can I get through to her if she has to be thinking of me first? Why would she think of her mom while snuggling with her boyfriend?"

We stand there in the falling snow, the helplessness almost tangible.

The sound of a sliding glass door draws our attention.

A large shape fills the doorway, silhouetted against the interior light.

"Hey, you two," a man's cheerful voice calls. "This snow is piling up. I hate to call it quits early, but Mindi, what do you say I take you home before the roads get too slick?"

Time seems to stop.

I know that voice.

Jackie's eyes lock on mine. "It's him," she whispers.

Kyle wasn't the killer.

It was his father.

Reif steps forward in alarm. "She can't go with him. Lorna, you've got to stop her!"

"I know!" I cry. "I'm trying!"

"Thanks Mr. Drummel." Mindi turns to Kyle. "My dad wanted me home earlier anyway. You coming too?"

"Mindi!" I shout, trying to grab her shoulders. "Mindi, you've got to listen. Don't go with that man! He's a murderer! Please, Mindi!"

"Sorry, Ky," his dad interrupts. "I've gotta run some errands, so I won't be home for a while. You don't mind if it's just you and me, do you, Mindi?"

Mindi flashes Kyle a pout. "I guess that's fine. I'll see you later this weekend though, right?"

"Sure. I'll text you tomorrow."

"Have a great Thanksgiving!" Mindi says airily as she follows Kyle's dad into the house.

"What do I do?" I scream in panic.

Jackie is completely unresponsive. I feel a twist of concern for her and what she must be feeling to see her killer face-to-face for the first time. To hear his voice again.

Reif notices Jackie's expression too. "Jackie, go back to the car. You don't need to be here for this. Go back to the Station and request another car to be sent for us. We'll come as soon as we can."

He reaches out to touch her on the shoulder and she jerks away as if startled.

I can't hang around to see if she obeys. I slip into the house and follow Mindi as she gathers her coat and purse.

"Mindi, listen to me. You've got to stop now. Call Dad. He said he would come get you. Don't leave with this man."

But Mindi makes no sign of hearing us. She gives a cheerful greeting to a thin woman with heavy makeup and perfectly coiffed hair standing in the kitchen. "Goodnight, Mrs. Drummel. Thanks for the treats!"

"Of course, dear," Kyle's mom says sweetly. "You're welcome here any time."

Reif comes into the kitchen and stands in front of Mindi. "Mindi! Listen to your mom. Don't go with this man!"

"Stop Mindi!" I cry. "You don't know who he is. You don't know what he's capable of. You don't know what he's done. Please, Mindi! Listen to me!"

"Goodnight, Kyle!" she calls as the front door shuts behind her.

Twenty-One

I feel trapped in a horrible nightmare, the kind I would have sometimes when I was mortal. The kind where I needed to run or yell and my limbs were like jello and my tongue felt like molasses. The kind where nothing I did could stop the catastrophe that was coming.

Reif and I sit in the back seat of Drummel's truck. The same truck where Jackie once laid on the floor crammed beneath the seats, her hands tied with zip ties. Even though I didn't see it, I can picture it as clearly as if she were right there with us.

Mindi sits in the front seat, fidgeting in that awkward way teenagers have with an adult they don't know well. They drive slowly through the streets of Billings. The snow is sticking to the road now, blinding white in the headlights. Few cars are out on the streets, leaving indistinct tracks that quickly fill in with fresh snow.

"Did you have a good time tonight?" Drummel asks politely.

"Yeah. Thanks for letting me come over." Mindi looks out the window.

"It's our pleasure. Is your dad waiting for you at home?"

"No, he's out tonight."

"Hmm." Drummel seems pleased by this. "Kyle sure likes you a lot. You're an awfully pretty girl, I guess you know."

"Um, thanks?" She says it like a question.

There's a long moment of silence before Drummel speaks again.

"Have you had sex with Kyle yet?"

"Excuse me?" Mindi looks at him sharply.

"Don't act so shocked. I was your age once too, you know. I knew what all the girls liked." He nods to her with a smile.

"Gross!" I hiss. "Don't talk to my daughter like that, you filthy pervert."

"With all due respect, Mr. Drummel," Mindi says, affronted, "I don't think that's any of your business."

"Kyle's my son. Of course it's my business."

"Yeah, but I'm not your daughter. Talk to Kyle if you want to know about his sex life."

He reaches over and puts his hand on her shoulder. "Come on, don't be like that."

"Please don't touch me, Mr. Drummel." Mindi shrugs him off. "No, we haven't had sex, all right?" She slouches against the door.

Drummel smiles knowingly and withdraws his hand. "Good, that's good."

I feel Reif's hand over mine. "Maybe he's smart enough not to try anything. Jackie was a random target. There are too many people who know that Mindi is with him right now."

"Or maybe he thinks he can get away with it because he got away with Jackie."

Drummel turns the truck onto a side street and Mindi sits up straighter.

"This isn't the way to my house," she says.

"I forgot something at the club today. Hope you don't mind. It'll just take a minute."

"I'd rather go home, actually." Mindi's voice is strained. At least she's getting the creep vibe. That's something. But is it enough for her to flee before it's too late?

Drummel waves her protest away. "We're almost there. It won't take long."

They pull into the empty parking lot and he accelerates, then slams on his brakes as they approach the curb so the back end of the truck fishtails and slides to a stop. Mindi yelps, grabbing the door to steady herself, and Drummel laughs.

"What an idiot," Reif growls.

"Just a bit of fun," Drummel says. "Don't get lost on me now," he says cheerfully as he slams the door shut and heads toward the entrance.

I slip up to the front seat next to Mindi, leaving Reif in the back. She's fidgeting with her phone.

"Mindi, can you hear me? Get out now, while he's

gone. Run to the nearest house and ask for help." I pour every ounce of love and concern for her into my words, desperate to be heard.

She looks over her shoulder toward the distant houses as if considering what to do. Her hand reaches for the door handle, but she pauses.

"Yes, go now while you can. You can reach one of those houses before he gets back."

Mindi releases the handle and reaches instead for her phone, thumbing quickly to her text messages.

Under the thread for "Dad" she sends a text.

coming home early, then adds, *lots of snow*

"He's coming back," Reif says.

Mindi sees him coming too and hastily types,

if I'm not home in 15—

Drummel opens the door and she sends the message without finishing it, then stuffs her phone back into her purse. He tosses a black duffle bag on the seat between them, right where I'm sitting. It would be in my lap if I were corporeal.

"See, just like I told you. Only a minute." He reaches over and slides his hand up her thigh. I try to push him away, but my hands go straight through him.

Mindi jumps and slaps his hand away. "I said not to touch me! Please just take me home now."

"You're a good girl, I can see that. The good ones are the most fun."

"Get out of here, Mindi!" I beg uselessly. "Go!"

Drummel scoots closer to her and reaches for her again, but she grabs the handle and pushes the door open. He grabs her coat and hair as she tries to jump out, and she falls with a yell against the running board. She pulls out of his grasp and lands on her knees on the hard pavement. Clambering to her feet, she slips in the slushy tire tracks and falls again. But Drummel is too fast. He lunges out of the cab and seizes her.

Her scream is cut off by his beefy hand over her mouth. She struggles to get free, but her boots have no traction and he's too strong.

"Don't be like that, Mindi," he says, his voice gentle. "What, do you think you're too good for me? You think you're saving yourself for someone special? You'll never find anyone as special as I am. I can show you things that most girls your age would only dream of."

Mindi continues fighting and trying to scream, her eyes wild with fear.

"Do you dream of me, Mindi?" he purrs into her ear. "I dream of you sometimes. Oh, those are nice dreams. I'm going to show you what I dream about."

"Reif! We have to do something to help her!"

"Tell me what to do, Lorna, and I'll do it!" Reif yells back, helplessness making him angry. "There's nothing we can do!"

Drummel throws Mindi back into the cab, face down on the seat. He climbs up behind her and rests a knee on her back to hold her still while he reaches for the duffle bag. He's massive, so much larger than his son. Mindi gasps from the pressure of his weight, struggling helplessly against him. Unzipping the bag one-handed, he pulls out long black zip ties.

"No," I murmur, Jackie's cries fresh in my memory. "Mindi, you've got to get away."

But he's too strong. He pulls her hands behind her and secures them, then follows with her feet. She kicks and squirms, but it does no good. Then he wrestles a handkerchief into her mouth and ties it tightly at the back of her neck, catching bits of hair into the knot.

When he's finished, he climbs back into the cab and shuts the door, crawling over Mindi to get to the driver's seat. He puts one hand on her head, keeping her face pinned against the seat as he looks nervously in the direction of the neighborhood on the far side of the parking lot.

"Since you decided to make a scene, we've gotta go somewhere else," Drummel grumbles, breathing heavily. "Just hold tight. I've got a great place. No one will bother us there."

He throws the truck into reverse and edges away from the curb. I crouch in front of Mindi on the floor of the cab.

"Come on, baby," I say desperately. "You've gotta get out of this somehow. I wish I could help you, but I can't. Somehow you've got to figure out a way."

Mindi kicks against the door. She gives a muffled yell, kicking at the handle with her feet, but her boots are awkward and clumsy and with her feet tied there's nothing more she can do.

Drummel palms her head with his gigantic hand. "Now, now. That's not going to help you. Be still."

But Mindi won't be still. She thrashes and kicks and tries to sit up. Drummel moves his hand to her neck and easily wraps his fingers around her throat. He squeezes and her feet still. Her eyes are wide with terror. He releases her just enough so that she gasps for breath, but he keeps his hand there as a threat, pinning her to the seat as he drives out of the parking lot and slowly down the street.

I want to shout and wake up the neighborhood, especially when Drummel raises his other hand to someone and nods in greeting, his knee keeping the steering wheel steady. Someone is out there, maybe walking their dog. Maybe putting out their trash. But someone is there, someone who could help, and they don't have any idea what's going on in the truck.

Drummel turns out of the neighborhood and winds through Rimrock Drive to the city limits. The snow is getting deeper, and the heavy tires are muted. All around us, homes glow cheerfully from the inside. But no one is venturing out into the weather.

As the houses give way to open ground, Drummel releases Mindi. She immediately kicks out again and the toe of her boot catches the door latch. The passenger door opens, flooding the interior with light as a warning bell chimes.

Drummel curses and swerves, grabbing the wheel with both hands.

Mindi slides away from him and pushes herself toward the door, but he's too fast. His large fingers wrap in her hair and yank, pulling her back down to the seat. I watch in horror as he strikes the side of her head hard with his fist. He hits her again, his face red and his lips wet. Mindi lays still.

The truck swerves again, the door slams shut, and the locks sound with an ominous click.

Mindi lays on the seat, her eyes glazed with pain.

Reif moves up from the back to join me. He nods to the truck bed with a satisfied expression.

"There's a toolbox back there. Not sure what all he's got in there, but probably something that would cut her zip ties."

He crawls under the seats, taking his time, then examines the underside of the dash.

"Ah. He's got a gun under the dash. A Ruger P89. It's hard to tell, but I'm guessing it's loaded. If Mindi can get a hold of it, does she know how to shoot?"

I sit on the floor of the cab, watching my daughter in pain. I don't answer.

"Lorna?"

I turn slowly to look at Reif. "What does it matter? We can't help her. He's going to do what he wants. She's going to end up like Jackie and there's nothing I can do to stop it."

Reif bites his lip but doesn't argue.

Tears form in Mindi's eyes and I wish I could cry as well. I feel hollow. Useless. I can't do anything for her, not until she dies and appears in the Arrival gate like Jackie did. Panicked and afraid. Burdened with the horror of what she went through.

But I will be there for Mindi. She won't be alone. And I'll stay with her now. She won't know it, and it will be hell for me to witness it. But in the worst moment of her life, I won't leave her alone.

I reach out and try to brush her hair with my hand. Her gentle sobs fill the truck.

"Ah, my sweet cupcake, don't be sad," Drummel says sweetly, sending a chill down my spine. "We're almost there. I'm gonna take good care of you."

He reaches under her coat and an expression of dark pleasure spreads across his face.

Mindi closes her eyes and her sobs increase, but with her arms pinned behind her, there's nothing she can do to stop his roving hand.

I want to look away. I don't want to watch him take pleasure in her pain. But for Mindy's sake, I stay with her. I stay focused on her eyes. Her beautiful gray eyes that don't deserve to see the things that she's about to see. Tears stream down her face and I reach as if to wipe them away and suddenly feel...something...

Just a flicker, but for a moment, my fingers almost feel wet.

Twenty-Two

I pull my hand away in shock.

"Reif," I whisper.

He looks at me, his expression stricken.

"I felt something. I think..."

I reach back toward her, but when I brush her face again, there's nothing.

"Come on, baby girl. I'm here. Can you feel me? Were you thinking about me? Is that why?"

The truck lurches as it pulls off the main road.

"I think we're almost there," Reif says.

"Where?"

"I don't know. I can't see anything out here in this snow. Just a minute."

He slips out of the truck and returns shortly.

"There's a little hollow ahead with what looks to be an abandoned farm. There's no house left standing, but part of the barn is still there."

The truck lurches to a stop and I look out the windshield. Snow blows sideways across the prairie, and in the headlights a structure looms out of the darkness.

Drummel looks down at Mindi with a flat grin. His eyes hold no feeling.

"All right, cupcake. We're here."

He gets out of the truck with a heavy sigh.

"Come on, Mindi," I say, my hand on her hair. "You've gotta think about me. Don't think about him. Think about me. I'm here. I want to help."

As soon as Drummel walks toward the front of the truck, Mindi jumps up and scrambles to the driver's side door. Desperately she tries to reach the power lock with her hands tied behind her back. Drummel lunges for the passenger door before she can lock it. He yanks it open and crawls in after her.

Mindi screams and kicks out at him with her bound feet. Her heel glances off his jaw and he staggers back. She turns back to the door, but there's nothing she can do with her hands bound.

Drummel grabs her with his massive arms. "You want to play rough, is that it? I was nice with the last one, but I don't have to be so nice with you."

Mindi is strong and athletic but he hauls her out of the truck easily, in spite of her thrashing. He carries her toward the collapsed barn as if she weighs no more than a small child.

"She was a sweetheart, she was. Her skin was paler than yours, like fresh cream. She was a virgin too, and oh how she cried. She cried and begged and it was just the sweetest thing."

Drummel skirts around to the back half of the barn

that hasn't collapsed. The side door and windows are missing and large gaps yawn between the wall planks, but it's mostly intact. I follow woodenly, refusing to leave my daughter but dreading what's to come. Never in my life—not when I got my diagnosis, not when when the scan showed the surgery hadn't worked, not when I transitioned and found myself forever separated from the ones I loved—have I felt such desperate helplessness. Reif joins me at my side, his arm around my shoulders.

Drummel throws Mindi to the floor, and she cries out in pain, scrabbling to get out of his reach. The headlights from the truck shine through the gaps in the wall, bars of light illuminating a filthy room that looks as if it was once a tack room but has since been left to teenagers with their graffiti and trash.

"Now, I've gotta go move the truck out of the way and get my bag. We don't anyone to see it from the road and interrupt us, do we? You stay here and I'll be right back. And just in case you think you want to run off, let me remind you that there's three inches of snow out there and I have a flashlight and you don't. You won't make it very far," he says with a low chuckle.

He disappears out the open doorway and Mindi collapses to the ground, trembling with fear. The headlights of the truck pull away and the room darkens, lit only by the reflected glow of the snow through the gaping doorway and a small window on the far wall.

I kneel in front of Mindi and place my hands on her shoulders. "Mindi, I'm here. I'm here to help. Can you hear me? Can you feel me?"

There it is again. A flicker of...something.

This time, Mindi starts in surprise.

"She felt something too!" I drop my hands and look up at Reif. "Reif! It's working!"

Reif looks at me in shock. "Lorna. You're...darkening."

I look at my hands. The familiar translucence is thickening. I look back at Reif and can't see him in the shadows. "Reif?"

And then a seismic shock rocks through me and I fall forward onto my hands and knees, gasping.

I am *gasping*.

Mindi yelps. I hear her scurry away and want to reassure her, but I can't. I can't move. So much feeling floods through me. Overwhelms me. Cold. So cold. The rough feeling of the dirty wood planks under my fingers. The biting cold of the air in my lungs. The stench of rot and decay filling my nose.

I am *alive*.

Somehow, I'm really here, in the mortal world.

And Reif is gone. Where he was before is empty darkness. Even the darkness is deeper somehow, my mortal eyes struggling to see in the dim light.

I push myself up to stand. So many senses badger me, it's hard to move. The feeling of my clothes against my skin. My hair brushing against my forehead. Even the beating of my heart. I look around.

"Mindi? Where are you?"

Mindi yelps in surprise. She tries to speak, but her gag muffles her voice.

I move forward slowly in the darkness, trying to find her. My leg brushes something substantial and I crouch in front of her. "It's all right. I'm not going to hurt you. I'm here to help. Let me take that off your mouth."

She stops pulling away and holds still while I reach to loosen the handkerchief. It's damp and smells of spit.

"Who are you?" Her voice is hoarse from screaming.

I pause. Can I tell her the truth? How can I explain? I don't know what rules I'm breaking to be here, but I know instinctively not to tell her the whole truth. At least not yet.

"I'm a friend. I'm here to help."

"Why are you here? How did you know—"

"It doesn't matter. I'll explain later. But right now we have to go before he gets back."

"He'll find me anyway."

"No, he won't. Let's find something to cut these zip ties."

"Oh please. They hurt so bad," Mindi says plaintively.

I pad around on the floor to see if I can find anything in the detritus collected in the corners that will work to cut through the plastic. I find newspapers and a few empty beer cans, as well as something that feels suspiciously like a dried human turd. But nothing sharp enough to cut the zip ties.

Suddenly I notice how silent it is.

The truck's engine has stilled.

"He's coming back," Mindi says in a panic. "He said he was was going to hide the truck, but now—"

"Shhh," I warn. "He doesn't know I'm here. We have the element advantage. If I help you, do you think you can walk? Or hop or something? Just so we can get you out of here. There's a toolbox in the back of his truck. We might be able to find something to get you free."

"I don't know. I can try."

I move to her side and grasp her by the arm, trying to help her stand. I have to get her out of here, but where can we go? With her feet bound, he'll outrun us. I saw how handily he carried her to the barn. With no weapon, he'll overpower us both.

It takes all of my strength to pull Mindi to her feet where she sways unsteadily.

"Sorry, my head...everything's spinning." She sags against me.

"It's okay," I say, but it's a lie. Nothing is okay. I'm almost as powerless as she is. I can't see any way to save her.

"Mindi, listen to me. We're going to have to find a place to hide. If I can get to the truck, then we can get away from him. But we have to find a place for you to hide first."

"You're leaving me?" she asks with a note of hysteria.

"No. I won't leave you, ever. But if we're going to get out we have to get to the truck. Which means you have to hide."

"But where?"

"Come with me." I tug her toward the darkest corner of the room where planks have been ripped away from the wall, exposing the center of the collapsed building. She shuffles awkwardly, her progress painfully slow even as she breathes heavily from fear.

We crawl through the gap, Mindi first with me following behind. Here the roof of the barn has caved in, leaving supports leaning precariously against each other. The snowy landscape outside casts a pale light through what remains of the walls and falls persistently through the open ceiling to cling to the broken wood and coat the frozen mud beneath us.

I grunt as I try to help Mindi over a splintery beam.

"I think I need to go under," she says.

"There's no room," I whisper. "We've got to hurry."

She heaves herself over, and I try to catch her. We both fall to the ground and I hit my head hard against a beam. Pain cracks through my skull and radiates down my spine. I feel sick with it and my vision wavers. I clamp my lips down against a cry.

We lay still in the silence, the sound of my breathing loud in my own ears.

"Do you think he heard us?" Mindi asks.

"Shh," I say shakily, blinking hard to clear my head.

Footsteps creak on the snow outside. I carefully ease out from under Mindi, my head brushing the offending beam again. I stifle the urge to whimper as my head throbs.

"Stay hidden," I whisper to Mindi. "I'll be back soon."

I crouch low, moving unsteadily back the way we came. Crawling back into the room, I hurry over to the door and squat low in the shadow below the window. My heart pounds furiously—it pounds!—and my breath is dangerously shallow, adrenalin making my limbs tingle. I try desperately to calm my breathing, parting my lips to alleviate the wheezing sound of it passing through my nose.

Drummel's bulk fills the doorway, and I'm freshly

aware of just how huge this man is. How near to danger I am.

Yes, I've succeeded in interacting with the corporeal world. But that means the corporeal world can also interact with me.

I don't fear him. I won't fear him as long as Mindi is in danger. But I need to be very, very careful.

"Where's my cupcake?" he says in a sing-song tone, the kind reserved for pets.

He steps into the room, mere inches from where I crouch. My heart races so fast with him near, I wonder how he can't hear it. The floorboards sag under his weight as he passes me. I slip behind him and to the outside, staying close to the wall under the eave where snow hasn't yet collected.

"Did you go and hide from me?" Drummel continues in an amused drawl. "That's too bad. Here we were getting along so well. Don't worry. I'll find you soon enough."

Twenty-Three

Staying low, I duck beneath the window and round the corner of the old barn. In the stillness of the night, Drummel's boots scrape against the floor. I let out a shaky breath as images fill my mind—images of Mindi trying to scuttle away from Drummel, like a trapped animal cornered by a predator.

I stifle a yelp as water drips down my neck from the overhanging eave. The snow casts a glow over the prairie, making it easy to see the truck's tire tracks. It looks like he followed the old farm road down a slope to a stand of trees. It's not far, but feels like miles away and I desperately pray that Mindi won't be found while I'm gone.

Snow swirls around me. It's so much colder than I remember. My little exercise jacket and yoga pants are doing nothing to keep out the blowing snow and wind. Instinctively I wish for a heavy parka, but to no avail. I'm stuck with these clothes.

I shiver and run faster.

Until I can't.

I've forgotten what it's like to run as a mortal. My legs burn and tire quickly. My heart feels as if it's going to burst out of my chest. And still I feel sluggish, the snow building up on my shoes and dragging my pace. The stand of trees draws closer with agonizing slowness.

When I finally reach the truck, bile rises in my throat and I choke it back down. Legs trembling, I grab the latch on the shell. Climbing shakily into the back of the truck, I find the toolbox that Reif described. There isn't a lock and I fish around in the dark, feeling past the screwdrivers and socket wrenches until my fingers close on the smooth shape of a utility knife.

Yes.

I gingerly feel to make sure there's a blade intact and then stuff it into my jacket pocket and climb back out of the truck.

Being able to pass through walls would be really handy right now.

My heart still pounds. My breathing is still uncomfortably fast. I cough from exertion.

Bodies are stupid.

The night is still, the only sound the rhythmic ticking of the truck's cooling engine. I try not to think about what Drummel will do if he finds Mindi. Perfect, innocent Mindi. And that monster is hunting her.

Hoping that she's still hidden, I throw open the door to the cab and paw under the steering wheel column. The handgun is strapped there, just as Reif said. What kind did he say it was? I can't remember but it probably wouldn't matter anyway. I don't know anything about guns beyond what I've seen on TV.

Just so long as it's strong enough to put a hole in Drummel.

My fingers shake as I grasp at the snaps and slide the gun out. It's heavier than I expect and I take that as a good sign. The metal is cold in my trembling hand.

"Calm down, Lorna," I say through gritted teeth. "You're likely to shoot Mindi if you can't settle down."

A scream drifts across the snowy prairie, piercing my heart.

He found her.

Praying harder than I've ever prayed in my life, I climb into the cab and reach for the ignition.

Keys. There is a God after all.

I turn the ignition, press on the gas, and the engine roars loudly in the empty night. Then I throw it into gear and the truck jumps forward. It's so much larger than the minivan I used to drive, and I have to perch on the edge of the seat so I can reach the gas, bouncing like a rag doll with each bump. Brush and young saplings rise up before me in the headlights and scrape like nails on a chalkboard against the sides of the truck.

As I emerge out of the stand of trees, I turn toward the barn. But I haven't gone far before sudden blackness yawns before me. I swerve, but it's too late. With a heavy jolt, the truck lurches to a stop. My head hits the door and I hiss through my teeth, tears springing to my eyes. I've forgotten how insistent pain is, so annoyingly demanding.

I push the gas pedal and the engine revs, but the truck doesn't move. I'm stuck.

Leaving the engine running and the headlights pointed up the hill, I grab Drummel's gun and clamber out of the truck. I barely register the wheel axel deep in a large hole before turning to the silhouette of the sagging barn at the top of the slope. A shape appears at the corner.

Drummel! I might have ruined our chance to escape, but at least I got him away from Mindi. Ducking out of sight, I crouch low and run back to the trees. If I can get to her before he finds me...

I don't finish the thought.

I hold the gun pointed toward the ground as I skirt around the trees, keeping them between me and the view from the barn. Drummel lumbers down the slope a lot faster than I would have expected for a man his size. I keep an eye on him, waiting until he disappears on the far side of the trees where I abandoned the truck.

Then I run.

The snow is wet and cold, and my clothes cling to my skin. My eyes haven't fully adjusted to the darkness again after the bright headlights of the truck, and I stumble over the uneven terrain. Snow coats my eyelashes and makes it even harder to see. It clings to my sneakers, making it feel as if I'm running on blocks. But running warms my body so after a few minutes I don't notice the cold anymore, except the iciness of my fingers grasping the gun. By the time I reach the top of the hill, sweat runs down my back.

I run into the barn as the truck door slams. Mindi is

barely visible in the corner, curled up in the fetal position. She holds one arm tucked against her protectively, and I wonder what he did to it as he dragged her back to the room.

"Here, love," I say gently. "Let me see your hands. It's okay. He's not going to touch you again. I'll make sure of that."

She doesn't answer, but she winces as she holds out her hands.

I slip the gun into my pocket and withdraw the box cutter to cut through the zip ties, then cut the binding around her ankles. In the distance, the truck revs uselessly. How long will it take him to get free?

Mindi scrabbles to her feet. "Can you get me out of here?" she begs, and the hope in her voice pierces my heart.

"I don't really...I don't have a car or anything."

"What? No car? How did you get here?"

"It's a long story," I say lamely.

"Do you have a cell phone? Can we call the police before he gets back?"

I blush as I realize I didn't even think to grab her phone while I was in the truck.

"I'm sorry. I don't have anything to help. Except this."

"Is that a gun?"

"We can't run," I say. "But we can be ready for him if he comes back."

I'm surprised that my voice doesn't shake. My blood is still pounding in my ears. My palms are clammy and my hands tremble. But I sound as calm as if shooting a man is no harder than helping Mindi fill out a college application.

"Where is he?"

"Chasing his truck."

Mindi makes a small sound. Is it a laugh or a sob? I'm not sure. I move closer to the door and examine the handgun. In the shadows, it's hard to see it clearly. I can't tell whether the safety is on or not. I'm not even sure which lever *is* the safety.

Suddenly I have to admit that I have no idea how to use it. Is it even loaded? Is this the kind that uses individual bullets? Or does it have a magazine or a clip or whatever it's called?

"Where are you when I need you, Reif?" I whisper in despair.

And then he's there, next to me. I jump as I feel his hand on my shoulder.

"It's about time you thought to ask for my help," he says with a smile in his voice.

"Ha! You're here!" I feel a surge of joy, but Mindi yelps from the corner. "It's okay, Mindi! He's my friend. He's here to help."

"How? Where did he come from?"

The sound of the truck engine changes, and headlights sweep the collapsed timbers as Drummel swings the truck around and heads our direction.

"He's coming. Help me, Reif. How do I work this?"

I pass him the gun. With deft fingers, he slides a cartridge out of the handle and nods.

"Plenty of rounds. Hollow point too, so they'll do some damage. That's good. Anything smaller and it wouldn't stop a big man like him. Are you sure you want to do this?"

"I...I don't know. I have to stop him. Think of what he did to Jackie! Someone has to stop him."

Reif slides the cartridge back into the handle and hands it back to me. "Safety's off. Just rack the slide and it'll be ready."

"Do what?" My hands are shaking.

The truck roars to a stop outside the barn, headlights blinding through the planks.

Someone grabs the gun from my hands.

"No."

I turn, expecting to see Mindi, but it's Jackie who stands there illuminated by the headlights, holding Drummel's gun. The look on her face is colder than the reflected snow.

"I want to do it."

"Jackie," I breathe. "I don't—"

"What do I do?" Her voice is hard.

Reif hesitates, then pulls back on the slide and it makes a clacking sound. "It's ready."

"Reif, she's just a kid—"

A shadow passes in front of the window.

"We've got to go, cupcake," Drummel says. "Someone's been here—" He enters the doorway and stops. Silhouetted against the light, I can't see the shock on his face as he registers the four of us, but I hear it in his voice.

"What in the name of—" he begins.

"Don't move!" Jackie screams, her voice shrill in the small space.

"Who are you? Is that my gun?" He takes a step forward and Jackie fires.

And misses.

The sound explodes in the small space, reverberating deep into my ears. Drummel ducks and pivots.

Jackie fires again.

And again.

And again.

With a grunt, Drummel stumbles against the doorframe. His weight tears the jamb from the rotting planks.

"That's enough," Reif says quietly, putting his hand over Jackie's. She stops firing and drops the gun, breathing heavily.

All is still. My ears ring painfully.

Drummel groans and slumps to the floor, grasping his side.

"I shot him," Jackie says, dazed.

I put my arms around her but I don't know what to say. She's warm and alive and I can hold her without either of us flinching.

"He'll live." Reif picks up the gun and points it at Drummel. He catches my eye. "Will you check the truck for his bag? Some zip ties would come in handy right about now."

I run to the truck—shying away from Drummel as I pass him—and grab both the zip ties and Mindi's phone. When I return, Jackie and Mindi are sitting together against the wall, vague shapes in the darkness.

"It's over," Jackie says soothingly. "You're going to be all right. He can't hurt you anymore. He won't hurt anyone anymore."

"I don't understand," Mindi says. "Who are you?"

Reif and I exchange a look.

"Don't worry about that right now," I say, handing her the phone. "You've got a couple of bars. Go ahead and call the police."

"Don't tell them about us," Reif warns. "Just tell them how you got here. Then say he had the gun with him. You found it in his coat."

"And the box cutter you found here mixed in with the newspapers," I say, taking it out of my pocket and wiping my fingerprints off of it. I don't even want to envision the mess it will cause for Mindi if her dead mom's fingerprints show up on it.

"But who are you?" Mindi persists, gathering her feet under her to stand. "How did you know I was here? How did you get here?"

I look at Reif. What can I say? If she doesn't recognize me, it won't do any good to tell her who I am.

Will it?

"We're friends of Jackie Renfro's," I say. "We've been watching him for a while, trying to figure out how to help the police track him down. When he took you tonight, well, we couldn't let him do to you what he did —" My throat closes with emotion.

Mindi looks at Jackie with eyes wide.

"I never believed in miracles before tonight. But you three—you're angels. And it's funny, but you kind of..."

She glances at me and then away, as if she's embarrassed to continue.

"Yes?" I ask breathlessly. Does she recognize me? "What were you going to say?"

"Just that...you kind of remind me of my Aunt Charley."

My little sister. I feel a wave of disappointment. "Really?"

"I know it's weird. Sorry."

"No, don't be sorry. That's...nice.

Reif squeezes my hand.

Twenty-Four

Drummel doesn't suffer silently. He holds his side and groans and swears in pain. At one point he even lunges for Reif, but Reif keeps Drummel's own gun trained on him and eventually he grows still. The girls and I move to the furthest corner of the barn with the newspapers and human excrement. I try not to think about what else we might find in daylight.

We sit with Mindi until sirens drone in the distance, coaching her on what to say. Reif comes up with a plausible story to explain how she got free. I'm prouder than ever that he was once Gerald Houston, the great crime novelist.

Mindi isn't in any hurry for us to leave.

"What if I say something wrong?"

"If you get the details wrong, they'll understand," Reif says. "You've had a very traumatizing experience. Some confusion is to be expected, but they won't be able to deny the evidence. Especially once they find his truck and link it to Jackie's murder."

I glance at Jackie. She's watching Drummel, and I wonder what she's thinking. Does she regret shooting him? Or does she wish her aim had been more deadly?

"Just remember," I say to Mindi, but my eyes linger on Jackie. "You're safe now. He can't hurt you anymore and when they're finished with their interviews, they'll direct you to people who can help. There are lots of resources to help you. Richard will fight for you to get whatever you need."

Mindi looks at me, startled. "How do you know my dad's name?"

"Old classmate," Reif says without skipping a beat. "Let's go. They'll be here soon and we don't want to confuse them with extra tracks."

"Right." I feel guilty leaving Mindi alone with Drummel. "You'll be okay?"

She nods, then leans against me for one final hug.

"I am so proud of you," I say with feeling. "You're a fighter. Don't forget that. You're going to get your life back, I promise. You're going to heal from this and your life will be yours again. You'll have power and no one will ever be able to take it from you again."

Reif touches my back gently to pull me away and places the gun on the floor next to Mindi. Approaching red and blue lights flash across her face. And with that, I leave my daughter again for the last time.

We slip out the door, careful to follow the wall so that we don't leave fresh footprints. The snow is falling so thick and fast that I can barely see where we walked earlier. By the time the police get out there with lights, it'll be too late to make sense of the multiple pairs of tracks. They'll be nothing but shapeless forms in the prairie landscape.

As we duck around the corner of the barn, out of sight of the police cars coming into view around Drummel's truck, I catch a glimpse of a dark SUV bringing up the rear. A door slams and I hear a voice that makes my heart leap into my throat.

"Mindi!" Richard calls.

I grab Reif's arm and turn back.

"Mindi!"

I can just make out his form moving through the police cars and the uniformed officer who blocks his path.

"Sir, I must ask you to get back—"

"What happened?" he asks desperately. "My daughter is here. I got a text and tracked her phone—"

"I'm sorry, but I must ask you to stand back. We're responding to a distress call and you can't—"

"Dad?" Mindi calls from the inside of the barn, her voice hopeful and full of emotion. "Dad, is that you?"

Richard leaves the officer and runs toward the barn. Instinctively, I shrink back into the shadows. I look at Reif, and he meets my gaze with a grim expression.

"Richard," I whisper. Richard is there, in the flesh. And so am I. A deep longing fills me and I move as if to go to him.

Then I see Reif's face and stop.

"What do you want, Lorna?" It's not a challenge. It's a plea.

What do I want? The answer is easy. I want my family. I want my life back. I want Richard and Mindi and Alex.

No, not so easy.

They aren't all I want.

I look at Jackie stomping her feet with cold, her hair tipped with snow. She blows warm air into her hands—hands that barely trembled as they stopped a murderer.

I look at Reif's clear blue eyes and the frown that creases his brow. No matter what I choose, they won't judge me. They love me. They came to help me when I most needed them. And maybe...just maybe...they need me too.

"I want to get out of the cold," I answer, turning my back on Richard and Mindi. My old life is lost to me, but I still have a future.

I reach for Jackie's hand as we walk, and she grips mine in return.

"Are you okay?" I pitch my voice above the blustering wind.

She nods but doesn't answer. Should I comfort her? Praise her? How terrified had she been to see Drummel in the flesh? Is she reliving those moments now? I can't possibly know. But I can hold her hand and reassure her that she isn't alone.

The wind cuts through my thin clothes and I shiver, my teeth chattering. Reif puts his arm around me. His touch feels comforting and familiar, but with a spark of something else. Something I've ignored for a long time. Something that makes me want to lean into him.

"I left the Vision car out there." Jackie gestures, her voice nearly lost over the wind.

We move across the prairie, our heads bowed against the driving snow. And then the snow isn't so cold, and my feet aren't so wet. The comforting weight of Reif's arm diminishes to a faint, dissonant hum.

"Look. It's over there."

Sure enough, a Vision car glimmers into existence in the night, its doors open and light spilling out onto the snow like a welcoming beacon.

Reif drops his arm. I feel warm and light and free again, no mortal body to tie me down. No body to bind me to the earth and the ones I love.

"I wondered if we would stay mortal," I muse. "But I guess it was never meant to be permanent."

Reif chuckles. "That would take a lot of explaining, wouldn't it? To show up alive in our late-20's when we are both very officially dead."

"I guess it's probably for the best to stay that way."

"Are you disappointed?" Jackie asks.

I look at her but it's Reif I'm thinking of when I answer.

"I'm not sure. Not really, I guess. Somehow I think I knew it wouldn't last. I didn't really have my hopes up."

"Oh," Reif says, his expression inscrutable.

"I mean," I say, reaching for his hand. "There are good things about being dead, right?"

Twenty-Five

The door to the Vision car slides closed, but the car doesn't move right away.

"Your Vision privileges have been revoked," the calm female voice says overhead. "You will not be returning to the Vision Station."

"What the...?" I shoot Reif a worried glance as the car starts moving.

"Why do I feel like I'm being sent to the principal's office?" he asks good-naturedly, but his eyes are shadowed with concern.

Jackie peers through the glass, trying to see out of the car. But, as usual, only indistinct colors and lights flash past.

We don't speak, the long minutes passing in worried silence.

When at last the car comes to a stop, I can see nothing outside the window. All is blank.

The door slides open and we stand motionless.

"Please exit the vehicle," the disembodied voice states.

Reif takes my hand and I take Jackie's and together we step out of the car.

"Where do you think we are?" I whisper.

"My worst nightmare," he murmurs.

"Huh?"

"All this blank white? It's like an empty sheet of paper taunting me to fill it with words. Writer's block hell."

I muster a wan smile.

With a purring sound, the car moves away and disappears.

In its wake stands a woman I recognize, though she looks...different. She's wearing a silvery gown that looks like it's made less of fabric and more light and motion.

"Teresa?"

She smiles her brilliant smile. "Hello, Lorna."

"Where are we? What's going on?"

"You've violated the laws that keep our world separate from the mortal world."

"I had to," I say indignantly, dropping Reif and Jackie's hands and stepping forward. "I had to save my daughter. If you knew what that monster was going to do—"

"I know. I know what would have happened if you hadn't intervened. Mindi would have suffered greatly, but then it would have been over. All her pain would have been gone. She would have joined you and then your joy would have been complete. You would have finally been able to pass on."

"No." I shake my head defiantly. "Not that way. I would rather she live a long life than join me like that. What would it have done to Richard and Alex? And how many more girls would that man have hurt? He had to be stopped."

"Instead," Teresa says as if I hadn't spoken, "Mindi will continue to live. She'll go to college and will be a bridesmaid at Richard's wedding next summer. But she'll have nightmares for years. She'll have a difficult time in relationships. She'll need therapy well into adulthood. But healing will come with time."

"Well that's more than I can say for what she would have gotten here," I snap, gesturing to Jackie. "Can you really tell me she would have been better off being ignored and passed over like Jackie was? Jackie who could never manage to find a counselor willing to take her case. Jackie who didn't even get a Greeter when she first transitioned. I don't know who's in charge here, but they're doing a pretty crappy job of taking care of the people who need it the most!"

Teresa's smile widens. "Jackie had a Greeter. She had you."

"Whatever. I'm no Greeter. I'm no counselor. But I'm all Jackie got because someone screwed up big time!"

"Jackie got you because you're exactly who Jackie needed. And because you needed Jackie."

I fume at Teresa, not sure what she's saying.

"She's right, Lorna," Jackie says, stepping forward. "You and Reif helped me in a way no one else would have. I couldn't have gotten here on my own, is that what you're saying?" she asks Teresa.

"Yes." Teresa nods. "And you helped Lorna too even though you didn't realize it."

"I don't understand," I complain. "Jackie was ignored. No one would help her—"

"*You* helped her. And that's who she needed. Jackie wouldn't have listened to a therapist assigned to her. But she trusted you. It was you who needed to help Jackie find her killer. It was you who needed to recognize the danger Mindi was in. And it was you who needed to figure out a way to save Mindi."

"I thought you just said that wasn't supposed to happen."

"No, I said that's what *would* have happened without you. But as soon as you decided to help Jackie, you changed things." Teresa beams. "Because you tried to help her, you figured out how to break the separation that divides our worlds."

"And brought us along with you." Reif grins with a wink at Jackie, who smiles warmly in return.

But I can't feel their same joy. "Why not just tell me this from the beginning? I feel like I've been tricked."

Teresa's smile fades. "I didn't know all this before. I didn't understand what was happening any more than you did. But I'm not sure it could have happened any other way. Think about it. If you'd known that Jackie's killer was going to target your daughter, what would you have done?"

"I would have hunted him down sooner and stopped him from taking her in the first place. Saved her from the next ten years of therapy."

"How could you have stopped him? The only way

that you crossed the barrier was because of your intense connection with Mindi in that moment. If she hadn't been afraid for her life, that connection wouldn't have been possible. It was only because she was in mortal danger that you could do what needed to be done. By stopping him, you opened the path for Jackie to start healing, and for you to heal as well."

Slowly, I start to see. Just a faint connection that comes together briefly with a flicker and is gone.

"I'm not sure I get it. But I think," I say haltingly. "I think I'm beginning to...if not understand, then at least hope that it will all make sense."

Teresa grins again. "Oh, it will. Your story is beautiful and rich and has so much more to come. Are you ready to begin?"

"What do you mean?"

"You aren't the first one who's crossed the barrier. It doesn't happen very often, but it does happen. We can't let you return and spread tales of what you've done. Otherwise everyone would be trying it for themselves and no one would be motivated to pass on."

I look at Teresa with her dress that moves like water and her glowing skin. "Is it worth it? Passing on? What if I say 'no?'"

"At this point, you don't have a choice. There's no going back now. You made your choice as soon as you defied the laws governing our world. So, are you ready to see what comes after this?"

I turn to Jackie, who watches Teresa with a kind of hopeful fascination. "What about you, Jackie? Are you ready? What if it's too soon for you?"

Her eyes shine with hope. I'm reminded of the photos of bright, optimistic Jackie we saw at her memorial. But this is more. She has a depth of wisdom in her brown eyes that takes my breath away.

"I think I'm ready," she says. "I don't feel the way I did before. Something happened tonight...I can't describe it, but I didn't kill him when I had the chance."

Reif shrugs. "Not for lack of trying."

She smiles sheepishly. "Okay, maybe I thought I wanted to. But I was relieved when I didn't. I stopped him, and now he'll answer for his crimes, and that's good. That means something. Like I'm stronger than I thought I was. Stronger than him, even."

I look at Reif and feel a stab of guilt. "And what about you? It's my fault you're here now. I dragged you into this mess, and now you have to pass on before you've finally learned to let go of coffee or whatever was holding you back. What if that causes problems later?"

Reif laughs, his eyes shining. "It wasn't coffee holding me back, Lorna."

"It wasn't?"

"No. Not coffee. Not my ex-wife. Not my alcoholism. Not my sorry excuse for a career."

"Um—"

"Hey, this is my monologue."

"Sorry. Then what was it?"

Reif steps closer to me and for a moment I almost feel as if I have a body again, the way I can imagine my skin tingling with his nearness. The shiver of anticipation running down my spine.

"It was meeting someone who gave me hope that I

could start fresh. Someone who believed the best in me. And it was being capable of loving her without fame or drink or ego or fear getting in the way. I couldn't pass on until she was ready to let go and move on herself."

His words...I'm so distracted by his blue eyes that they don't make sense. It takes several long breaths to sort them out.

"You mean me?" It's almost a whisper.

"I mean you," he says.

I'm seized with a desire to feel his arm around me the way I did in the mortal world. But when I reach for his hand, there is still the same uncomfortable buzzing. Yet our hands hold a sheen that wasn't there before.

"Is this...okay?" I ask Teresa.

She nods. "Winston and I have talked a lot. He gave Reif a little more leeway than usual trying to help move things along. To help you see clearly what was before you. But eventually you got there on your own."

I remember my last letter to Richard, and the feelings I had when I turned away from him at the barn.

"Yes, I guess I did."

As I look into Reif's eyes, it seems as if all the joyful moments of his life are right there before him. And maybe they are. With my other hand, I reach for Jackie's, and I wonder if my eyes are shining quite like hers. The light in both of their eyes seems to make their whole faces glow, only it isn't so bright that I have to look away. It envelops me and I want to join them.

Together, their hands in mine grow solid and firm—warm and real—as we prepare to face what comes after.

Thank you for reading!

I hope you've enjoyed this adventure through the afterlife. If so, please consider leaving a review on Amazon or Goodreads. (Or both for you overachievers!) Thanks for helping get my work into the hands of other readers like you.

Looking for more clean suspense with characters you'll fall in love with?

Readers everywhere have been losing sleep with *Smoke Over Owl Creek*, a gripping tale of atmospheric suspense exploring the darker side of small town life. The first of a three-book series, its twists and turns will keep you turning pages late into the night.

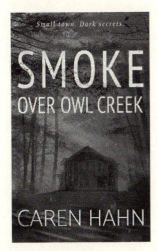

THANK YOU FOR READING!

And—because I aim to please—here's an excerpt to give you a preview:

It wasn't a baby.

Val's head snapped up. She blinked to clear her vision, her hand limp against her book. For a single heartbeat, she tried to make sense of her surroundings. The clock on the nightstand read 1:40 am, and she vaguely realized she must have just drifted off.

The bedside lamp cast long shadows against the faded wallpaper, stained and bruised from years of use. As she reached to shut it off, the thought came again.

It wasn't a baby.

Val sat up, alert. She threw back the sheet, slipped her bare feet into a pair of flip-flops, and hurried to the door. Heart pounding, she moved down the stairs as quick as she dared, the flip-flops making a slapping sound against the aged wood. The air was sharp with the scent of smoke. Moonlight shining through a large window on the landing illuminated her way to the back of the house. The outside porch light made the small panes of stained glass in the Victorian-era door glow in tones of amber, blue, and emerald. The heavy door protested when she pulled.

A cool breeze greeted her bare arms and legs as she stepped outside; a fresh contrast to the stuffy house. With a brief glance, Val took in the yard, her eyes drawn to the shadows under the trees. Keeping one eye on the darkness, she ran to the lump on the trampoline.

Abby's hair was just visible above the blankets, the rest of her burrowed deep for warmth.

Val stroked the thin blond curls.

"Hey, sweetie," she murmured. "Let's go inside."

If Abby were smaller, Val could have scooped her up in her arms and carried her to the house. But she was seven now, and big enough that Val wouldn't have made it more than a few steps.

"Come on, baby. I need you to wake up. I want you to sleep in the house tonight."

With gentle prodding, Abby finally stirred.

"You said I could sleep on the trampoline," she accused, her words slurred with sleep.

"I know, but I changed my mind. I don't think it's a good idea." Val looked back toward the shadows where the line of trees marked the rise of the mountain behind the house.

Earlier that day, while Abby had been playing on the rusty swing set, Val had been indoors packing away some of her parents' old stuff to make room for the boxes she and Abby brought with them when they moved in. The rhythmic squeal of the swing set chain was a soothing accompaniment to the childhood memories reawakened by each book, each card, each photo she unearthed.

At some point in the afternoon, she'd heard the distant sound of a wailing baby drifting over the dry fields. The Parkers lived down the hill and across the road, and in the full foliage of summer, she could barely make out the roof of their barn through the trees. She'd assumed they had family visiting with children and hadn't thought anything of it.

Until in her sleep, she remembered the Parkers were out of town.

Yet there was something else that could sound hauntingly like a screaming child.

Would she know if a cougar watched her now? She felt a chill on her neck at the thought. Keeping an eye on the dark line of trees at the edge of the yard, Val shushed Abby's protests and helped her down from the trampoline. When her feet hit the dry grass, Abby yelped.

"I've got a sticker in my foot."

"We'll fix it in the house."

"But it really hurts."

"Let's get inside first."

Her arms full of blankets, Val helped Abby hobble across the yard, supporting her daughter's weight. She couldn't shake the feeling that something was watching her from the shadows. But the light from the porch blinded her to the darkness under the trees. The yard seemed so much bigger in the dark, the safety of the house far away.

She restrained a sigh of relief when they reached the porch. The old door squealed against the frame as she pushed it open. It stuck worse now than it used to.

She turned around as she closed the door, taking one last look at the yard. There, under the distant trees, she saw a faint patch of...something.

She blinked, her eyes straining.

There was a smudge of something not-quite-shadow. As she watched, it dissolved into the darkness.

Join Val's heart-pounding adventure in *Smoke over Owl Creek* today. (Apologies in advance for any sleep deprivation incurred. #notsorry)

Acknowledgments

My sister, Crystal Brinkerhoff, explains her inspiration for writing horror quite simply: "I tap into my own fears and then exploit them."

I don't write horror, but way back in 2017 when I first decided to write a suspense novel, I reflected on my own fears to see if I could find an interesting theme. I wasn't about to tackle spiders or uniform holes (look up trypophobia if you're curious). But having lost a beloved sister to cancer only a few years earlier, it didn't take long to settle on a more compelling and primal fear—death. Specifically, dying young and leaving the business of raising a family unfinished.

That's when the concept behind *What Comes After* was born.

All of my work draws from personal experience in some way, and the same is true of *What Comes After*. Grief at losing my sister when I expected to make memories with her far into our old age. Struggling to relinquish control as my children age and need freedom to grow. Frustration over not being able to solve crimes without a body.

Okay, maybe not that last one.

As an aside, I consider myself a very religious person,

and my life is deeply informed by my beliefs about the afterlife. This story, however, is not that. Consider it more of a thought experiment than a doctrinal thesis. It was fun to imagine an afterlife where the dead have to work through whatever trauma they've carried with them before being able to progress to something better. It definitely made me think about the mechanics of life and death more than I ever had before!

Special thanks go to Crystal Brinkerhoff and Rachel Stauffer who saw the first draft and helped make the ending stronger. Jenny Hahn and Cori Hatch provided valuable feedback as beta readers, and Rachel Pickett's editing skills raised it to another level.

I'm especially grateful to Andrew, my partner of twenty-four years, who has stood by my side through thick and thin. I'm so glad I can spend my before and after with you.

About the Author

CAREN HAHN specializes in relationship-driven fiction featuring empathetic characters who are exquisitely flawed—the stuff of great book discussions. She graduated from Brigham Young University where, between courses on Humanities, English Lit, and Biblical Hebrew, she squeezed in as many Creative Writing classes as she could. Caren lives in the Pacific Northwest with her husband and six children.

Sign up to get updates at carenhahn.com and receive a free collection of short stories. Follow her on social media to learn more about her upcoming projects.

Made in the USA
Columbia, SC
28 November 2022